An
Advanced
Degree in
MURDER

Denise McDonald

PAGE PUBLISHING, INC.
Conneaut Lake, PA

First originally published by Page Publishing 2021

ISBN 978-1-6624-2886-9 (pbk)
ISBN 978-1-6624-2887-6 (digital)

Printed in the United States of America

For Mom and Dad. Endless support, endless encouragement, endless love.

1

I was speaking to a lecture hall full of new freshmen when the homicide detective called. Back in my office after my Psychology 101 class, I checked voicemail to find a message from my college roommate's younger brother. I knew said brother had become a cop, but last I'd heard, he was working burglary and theft. It seemed that little bro had earned his gold shield and graduated to Robbery-Homicide. Good for him. But why on earth did he want to talk to me? I picked up the phone and was starting to punch in his number when a student knocked on my open door.

"Professor McKennitt?"

Office hours. Detective Malone would have to wait.

"Come on in," I said, replacing the handset and gesturing to the chair in front of my desk. "What can I do for you?"

He shuffled in, sat down, and dropped a backpack that must have equaled a third of his body weight. I resisted the impulse to tell him to pick up his feet, recalling my mother's most oft-uttered directive when my brothers and I were teenagers.

I've been teaching at a university for twenty years, but each incoming freshman class looks so much younger than the last. Here are these kids, many of them away from home for the first time, trying to get used to college-level classes and navigate dorm life, wondering when the "fun" they've heard so much about will begin. My student was carefully looking at everything in the office but me. It seemed cruel to wait it out, so I prompted.

"How can I help you?"

He finally looked at me. Baby steps.

"Um, Professor…so you said we have to sign up for a research project with a grad student…"

"That's right. Grad students need test subjects, and freshmen should really see what it will be like if they choose to major in psychology. So you help each other out. Is there something confusing about that?"

He was looking at the floor again.

"Um…it's just that…I have a full class load, and with all the reading and the homework…and having to do my laundry, when am I going to have time to be a research subject?"

His laundry. Poor thing, this one had clearly never been away from home before.

"Well, I think you'll find that whichever project you sign up for won't actually take up that much of your time. And you may well end up with some practical experience that will help with one of your projects later."

That freaked him out.

"*My* projects?"

"Down the line. *Way* down the line. Let's just concentrate on this semester, shall we? Tell you what, sign up for a project, meet with your grad student, and then come back and talk to me about it. If you really think you won't have time, we can figure something out, okay?"

His shoulders lifted, and the ghost of a smile appeared.

"Really? That would be great. Thanks, Professor McKennitt!"

"Sure thing. Believe it or not, I'm on your side."

That earned me an actual smile as he stood and shouldered the enormous backpack. He'd either look like a gym rat or be a chiropractic patient by the end of the semester. A few more freshmen and a grad student dropped by, leaving me with less than fifteen minutes to discover why Caitlyn's brother had called me before I had to go to a department workshop.

The good detective picked up on the first ring.

"Homicide. Malone."

"Hello, Detective Malone, this is Ashley McKennitt returning your call."

"Hi, Ashley, uh…Professor. Thanks for getting back to me."

"Of course, and call me Ashley. I have to say I was surprised to hear from you. It's not every day I get a call from a homicide cop, which raises the question, why *did* you call me?"

His tone changed. I could hear a hint of the kid I'd met when Cait and I began our sophomore year.

"Well, I was hoping I could buy you a cup of coffee and pick your brain."

"About?"

"I'd rather tell you in person."

Color me intrigued.

"Okay, Detective, consider my curiosity piqued. I've got full days tomorrow and Wednesday, but my first class doesn't start until ten Thursday morning."

"Thursday is good. Do you know that little café in East Sac next to the old hardware store?"

"I do. It's just a few blocks from my house."

"Good deal. Eight o'clock?"

"You got it. I'll see you then."

We said our goodbyes, and I gathered my notes and then set off across campus to one of the psych department workshops I'd signed up for, still wondering what the hell a homicide cop thought he could learn from me.

I suppose an introduction is in order. My name is Ashley McKennitt, but I'm Ash to those close to me. I'm forty-eight years old, currently single, and, for the past eight years, have been a professor in the psychology department at my alma mater, California State University, Sacramento, where I earned my bachelor's and master's degrees. After taking a year off to tag along with my then-boyfriend and his band as they toured Europe, I went to UC Berkeley and completed my PhD. I'm a native Californian, born in a little town in the mountains southeast of Los Angeles but have been in the northern part of the state since my late teens.

Sacramento is a very undemanding place to live. The pace is slower than that of Los Angeles or the Bay Area, the cost of living is reasonable, and the traffic is manageable for the most part. The city has more trees per capita than Paris, and we have the benefit of the Sacramento and American rivers to improve our scenery even more. We're pretty much equal distance away from the Bay Area, Tahoe, and the wine country proper, plus we're surrounded by boutique wineries in El Dorado Hills, Clarksburg, and Lincoln. I'll likely never work for the Chamber of Commerce because my first slogan suggestion would be, "Sacramento, close to all the cool stuff."

When my ex and I split and sold our house, I was able to put a down payment on my dream home in East Sacramento, a neighborhood I'd thought was out of reach. After nearly three years, I still get a little thrill when I turn onto my street and think, *This is where I live.* The market has since gone crazy, and people in my income bracket have been priced out of the area. My "noncommute" to campus is less than three miles and doesn't require getting on the freeway. Should that ever change, I'll likely have to upgrade to a newer car that gets great mileage, but for now, my 1966 Mustang gets me where I need to go and still makes me incredibly happy to own.

For the past two years, I've shared my house with a rescue dog named Cody, who is border collie and I'm not sure what else—maybe shepherd, husky, or both. He's great company, loves our morning runs and hikes in the foothills, and is an excellent watchdog. When the tule fog settles in to stay during the winter, it can get a little bleak in the valley, and if you can't stand the thought of triple-digit temperatures in the summer, the capital city might not be for you. But most of the year, the weather is quite nice. Each summer brings a few sweltering nights when the mercury refuses to fall, and I wonder if I should think about moving. Then the delta breeze comes to the rescue, and I sit on my back patio with the dog, wondering why I would ever live anywhere else.

2

I parked down the block from the café, and as I got closer, the aroma of freshly brewed coffee became stronger. I wasn't sure I'd recognize Detective Malone, as we hadn't seen each other in several years, but I spotted him immediately upon walking through the door. Although six years younger, Jesse looks enough like his sister to be her twin. I approached the table he'd claimed amid the morning rush, and he stood. Nice. Old-fashioned manners never fail to impress me.

"Ashley," he said, shaking my hand, "it's good to see you. It's been a while."

"Yes, it has, and it's good to see you, too, Detective Malone."

"That's enough of that. Call me Jesse. You've known me since before my voice changed."

I smiled. "Fair enough. Jesse it is."

Once we were back at the table with our caffeinated beverages of choice, we spent a few minutes catching up on Cait. She and I have remained close friends since our college days, but her journalism career kept her busy and, quite often, out of the country. I glanced at my phone to check the time, and he got the hint.

"Okay, I know you have to keep an eye on the time, so here's the deal. Since I'm the FNG, uh, freakin' new guy on the squad, I got stuck with a cold case, a two-year-old murder that I've gotten nowhere with. Last week, there was a homicide in the park by the river."

"I heard about that," I said, still wondering why I was there.

"I think the two cases are connected. I can't really explain why, and I can't very well go to my captain with a gut feeling."

"I'm still not sure what you think I can offer," I said, toying with my cup. "Surely you have a department psychologist."

He nodded. "We do, but thanks to budget cuts, she splits her time between us and Yolo County, and like I said, I'm the newbie, so I'm low man on the totem pole. I might have to wait weeks to talk to her. Besides, I want a fresh perspective. I think you can offer a non-cop take on psychopathic behavior and the criminal mind."

Wow. "Well, I can't claim to be an expert on criminal behavior."

"But you know much more about mental aberrations than I do."

"That may be true, but…can you even do this? Can you talk to a private citizen about an open investigation?"

He looked out the window and slowly let out a breath. "I may be treading into a gray area," he said, turning back to me, "but I am able to consult with experts who aren't employed by the department. And it's not like I'm going to take you to a crime scene or endanger you in any way."

My turn to look out the window and try to breathe. This was quite a surprise.

"Will you at least give it some thought, Ashley? You don't have to decide right now. Think about it this weekend. I realize a murder investigation isn't something to take lightly, and I assure you I understand the gravity of what I'm suggesting. But if you end up helping, think of the research paper you could publish."

Oh, little brother was good.

"Okay, Detective, let me give it some thought, and I'll get back to you. But right now, I've got to get to class."

"I need to get going too," he said, getting to his feet. He handed me a business card and said to call him anytime. I thanked him for the coffee, and we walked out into the late summer sunshine. A murder investigation. *Two* investigations, actually. Just another day in the life of a college professor, right? Had I any idea what I was about to get myself involved with, I would have tossed Jesse's card and walked away right then. But what they say about hindsight is all too often true.

3

I love my job. I'm much more at home at a state college than I'd be at an Ivy League school, and psychology is a good fit for me. But as much as I enjoy teaching psych classes and working with grad students, the best thing about this gig has been getting approval to teach a class called Popular Culture and Societal Trends, which is exactly what it sounds like. That's right, I get paid to talk to my students about music, movies, books, art, and television. Being a pop culture junkie does really pay off at times. At this point, the class is only offered in the fall, but as it fills up immediately, with very few dropouts, there's talk of adding it to the spring class lists as well. The textbook is a self-published adaptation of a paper I presented while completing my doctorate. Something that would never happen somewhere like Stanford or Princeton.

Eager to begin my favorite class, I walked into the room and smiled. I know it has more to do with the subject matter than me, but there's nothing like seeing a room full of students eager to hear what you have to say. I started with my usual opening remarks about the course and was surprised to see a hand go up right away.

"Yes?"

A tall, lanky guy wearing cargo shorts and a faded T-shirt squirmed a bit and then said, "Uh, Professor McKennitt? I heard that you'll fail anyone who disses the Beatles."

His classmates stared at him, and I heard a nervous giggle. So that was the word on campus? I suppressed a smile.

"Regardless of what you may have heard, I'm always open to a civilized, respectful discussion. Of course, we're all going to have different tastes, and how boring would it be if everyone liked the same things, right?" I looked around the room, heard murmuring, and saw a few smiles.

"But let me say this—if anyone wants to tell me the Beatles are overrated, he or she had better be prepared to name a musical hero who didn't learn everything they know from John Lennon or Paul McCartney."

That got their attention. Nothing like setting a few ground rules early in the semester, rule number one being, *do not diss* my *musical heroes.*

"So just keep that in mind, and we're good." I smiled and was rewarded with a few tentative grins. I had a feeling this was going to be a fun group.

"Okay, I'm going to assume that you've read the course description and are here because you share my opinion that art—and I'm using that term broadly here to encompass all artistic pursuits, from visual arts to music, writing, movies, and television—can change attitudes, affect social conventions, and most certainly make the world a better place. Are there any general questions about this course?"

A few hands went up.

A petite redhead in the front row asked, "Will we listen to music in class?"

"Absolutely, and it won't just be what I decide to share."

The guy who asked about the Beatles wanted to know if we'd be watching movies.

"Most likely not because we can't devote that kind of time to any one movie, but we will view and talk about specific scenes that have become part of our cultural consciousness, like the horse head in the bed from *The Godfather* or the tears in rain monologue from *Blade Runner.*"

We spent the rest of the class discussing how quickly attitudes can change regarding what's risqué and should be censored and, more importantly, who should get to make those decisions. The open-mindedness of young people continues to give me hope for the future. With September being Banned Books Month, I always circulate the current and most-frequently banned lists and then watch the incredulity sink in. *To Kill a Mockingbird? The Color Purple? Harry Potter?* The lists are a great icebreaker for the beginning of the semester and always result in a lively discussion. Students end up wanting to participate in Banned Books Week events at local bookstores and organize their own events on campus. Last year, two of my students wanted to stage a mock book-burning à la *Fahrenheit 451* in the main quad. I sincerely doubted that the university would allow it but encouraged them to put together their proposal and take it to the dean by way of the department chair first, who looked at me as though I'd completely lost my mind. The proposal was rejected, whether for the idea in general or the fact that in the interest of being authentic, the women planned to have a Bible as part of their event, I was never sure. And yes, we did spend an entire class period discussing the irony of an event to protest censorship being denied. Although I was disappointed for the class, that's one of those life lessons I couldn't have illustrated better.

4

T he fall semester at Sac State begins in late August. Students show up for class dressed as though they're headed to the river, and instructors pray the AC won't fail. After that first week, we're treated to the long Labor Day weekend, and then it's time to buckle down and get to work. September had begun with the usual heat we see in the valley, but the mornings were pleasantly cool. As Cody and I set off on our run through nearby McKinley Park the morning after I met with Jesse, I continued to think about his intriguing invitation to be a part of his investigation. When the park opened in 1871, it was privately owned and known as East Park, given its location in a then-undeveloped area to the east of the city limits. After the assassination of President McKinley, it was renamed in his honor and eventually became a city park, which boasts a duck pond, playgrounds, a pool and tennis courts, as well as walking/running trails and a beautiful rose garden, which is a prime location for outdoor weddings.

We'd reached the park and started on our habitual route when I decided a good, old-fashioned pro and con list might be the only way to determine what to do about Detective Malone's offer to serve as a consultant. Cody trotted happily alongside me, enjoying being on the move and blissfully unaware of the dilemma I was pondering. On the pro side, I was being asked to lend my professional expertise to a detective. I would no doubt have access to information and gain insights into the criminal mind that few in academia could hope for, and such an experience would provide rich fodder for a research paper. Those were three extremely solid pros. As far as cons, I started with the fact that it was a *murder* investigation. I'm not squeamish by nature, nor do I go through life pretending bad things never happen, but a few undergrad criminal justice classes were the closest I'd come to delving into that world. If I were to agree to be a part of the investigation, I'd be in for a crash course on the ultimate cruelty my fellow humans are capable of.

Running along the path near the pond, I nodded greetings to my fellow joggers while Cody kept an eye on the ducks. He'd still be at my side off leash, but I knew how much he'd love to rush the flock and jump into the water. I thought it was about time to take him to the river again to indulge his water dog tendencies. We'd have at least another three weeks or so of warm weather. We veered away from the pond, and I got back to my mental debate. Though much less intense at a state university than the Ivy League, *publish or perish* was still something I had to contend with. And the fact was, I'd not come up with anything new to tackle since my last paper. This really was a once-in-a-lifetime opportunity.

Rounding the corner onto my street, we slowed to walk the last block home. Though I'd only managed to come up with one con, it felt pretty weighty—it might even equal the three pros. And yet... when would I ever encounter an opportunity like this again? I let us into the house, unclipped Cody's leash, and watched him make a beeline for his water bowl in the kitchen. Filling a glass with water for myself, I realized the pro and con list was just a detour; the decision was already made. I poured kibble into Cody's bowl, went into my office to find Jesse's card, and dialed his number.

After an uneventful day of lecturing and classwork, I drove out to the Sacramento Police Station near the Executive Airport. I checked in with the front desk clerk and picked up a visitor's badge. The clerk buzzed Jesse and invited me to wait on a bench across the room. Detective Malone appeared a few moments later to escort me to a conference room down a long hallway.

"Thanks for coming in, Ashley. I know you have mixed feelings about this. I'm going to share what I've been authorized to from the murder book, including photos. If at any time you want to bail, just tell me and that will be it. No one is going to make you do this."

"Thanks, Jesse. I appreciate that. I think I'm up to it, but I haven't seen actual crime scene photos before, so I can't promise that I'm going to be able to handle this."

"Understood. I'm just grateful that you're willing to give it a shot."

We went into a small conference room with glass doors.

"The department is all about transparency these days," he quipped.

We sat down and Jesse said that his partner, Detective Eduardo Marquez, was in court but that I'd be able meet him the next time I came to the station. He placed a binder in front of me, explaining that it contained the particulars of the cold case he'd been working, an unsolved murder from nearly two years ago.

"You don't need to get bogged down in the details, so I'll give you a quick synopsis."

He went on to say that a thirty-five-year-old White male was found in his car with what initially appeared to be a self-inflicted gunshot wound to the head. A .38 caliber pistol lay in his lap. The car was parked at the old sports arena on Del Paso Road and not discovered for twenty-four to forty-eight hours after the death. The investigating officers were ready to declare it a suicide when one decided there was something odd about the location of the entrance wound. The forensics team agreed and said the guy would've had to bend his wrist at an impossible angle to achieve the trajectory the bullet took on the way out.

"So it was deemed a homicide, and here the case sits, growing colder every day," Jesse said. "If you're ready, I can show you the photos, but I want to warn you that the bullet used was a hollow point, which has what we call a mushrooming effect as it leaves the body. That means it flattens out and creates a much larger exit wound than a regular round."

Yikes. Why the hell did I agree to this? I took a deep breath and detached from the situation, telling myself this was no different from countless clinical studies I've been involved with. I nodded to let Jesse know I was ready.

He opened the binder and extracted three black and white photographs taken from different angles. The first one was from the passenger side, and apart from the bullet wound behind the man's ear and the blood on the driver's side window, it wasn't particularly gruesome. There was pistol in his right hand, which was resting in his lap on top of a newspaper. The next photo was taken straight on through the windshield and revealed that a fair portion of the left side of the man's head was missing. My sharp intake of breath made Jesse ask if I was okay. I nodded, not quite ready to speak.

"The last one is the worst. You can skip it if you'd like."

I shook my head. "No, I'm okay."

The final picture was taken from the driver's side of the car and showed the exit wound in gory detail. Jesse put the photos back into the binder and set it aside, and I remembered to breathe. He brought me a cup of water from a cooler in the corner of the room. I thanked him, and he asked if I was ready to go on to the new case.

"Yes," I said, more to myself than him.

Jesse reached for another binder, explaining that homicide officers refer to the case file created during an investigation as a murder book. The file includes crime scene photographs and sketches, as well as forensic reports, notes from the autopsy, investigators' notes, and witness interviews. It captures the complete paper trail of a murder investigation and creates a time line from when the murder is first reported through the arrest of a suspect.

"A little over a week ago," Jesse began, "two women out for their morning run found a man slumped over a picnic table in Discovery Park. They assumed he was a homeless guy until they realized he was wearing clean slacks and a dress shirt. They went to get a closer look and saw blood all over the table, so they called it in."

While laying the photos in front of me, Jesse explained that the man, a forty-nine-year-old Hispanic, had multiple stab wounds, none of which were deemed fatal, suggesting that the killer had toyed with the victim before slitting his throat. The photos showed the man sitting on the bench with his head on his folded arms, resting in a pool of blood on the table. The killer had used the man's blood to paint the letters *A* through *E* above his head. How random, weird, and extremely creepy. There was something under the victim's right arm, but I couldn't tell what it was.

"What's under his arm? Is that another newspaper?"

"No. It's a picture from one of those paint-by-number kits."

"Are you serious? Do they even make those anymore?"

"Someone must, or maybe our killer had one from his childhood stashed in Mommy's attic. But you've hit upon what makes me believe we might be looking at the work of the same sicko. I think the newspaper and the painting kit could be his calling cards. They have nothing to do with the victims and are completely out of place. I don't think the first guy drove out to the arena to catch up on the news, was surprised by the killer and offed. This guy was not sitting in the park painting in the wee hours of the morning when his number came up, so to speak."

I don't have much of a background in criminal behavior, but I do know quite a bit about psychosis, and Jesse was correct about calling cards. Murderers who kill for sport as opposed to those who commit crimes of passion often feel the need to take credit for their deeds and leave some sort of marker. Sometimes it's just a "Hey, look what I did" statement, and sometimes it's a challenge to the cops, like, "Bet you can't catch me."

"This is what I really wanted your take on, Ashley. The department shrink is spread so thinly between us and the West Sacramento office that I still haven't been able to talk to her. I need to have a well-reasoned theory backed by solid facts before I can take this to the captain. I'm new to homicide and I know I might be charging off in the wrong direction here, but my gut is telling me to follow this thread as far as it goes. And like I said, if this is too much for you, say the word and you're out."

"I appreciate that, but I'm in. I can't promise I won't be squeamish at times, but I have to admit I'm intrigued. Needing to know the why and to understand what it is that makes people act like they do is what initially drew me to psychology."

"Okay then. Welcome aboard, partner."

Jesse explained that photos, sketches, or any other information from the murder book couldn't be taken out of the station.

"Anything I can share with you will have to be done here."

"I'm okay with that."

He smiled. "I have a hunch that we're going to make a good team, Professor McKennitt."

"I believe you're right, Detective Malone," I said, returning the smile.

Jesse escorted me back to the lobby, where I returned my visitor's badge and we said our goodbyes.

5

Walking out to my car, I thought about graduate school and how much I enjoyed clinical research. At one point during my second year, I had an opportunity to pursue a forensics path, which could potentially have led to a position within a police department, but opted for neurolinguistics instead, being a word geek at heart. From there, I branched out to cognitive psych, as I was especially interested in focusing on language use, memory, and perception, and after earning my doctorate at Cal, I took my first teaching position at San Francisco State. I then ended up back in Sacramento. And now, thanks to this latest twist of fate, almost twenty years later, none other than my college roommate's brother was drawing me into the criminal justice world. Life is funny that way.

I'd first met Jesse when Cait and I moved into the dorms at the beginning of our sophomore year. He was a skinny, tall-for-his-age thirteen-year-old with big blue eyes and a sweet smile. His sister spoke of him often, and despite their age difference, they've always been close. Cait and I remained best friends after going our separate ways once we'd earned our bachelor's degrees. I went on with school, while she went out into the world and launched what turned out to be an extremely successful career as an investigative journalist. Also a skilled photographer, her work has graced countless magazine covers. Three years ago, she won a Pulitzer. She'd kept me apprised of Jesse's accomplishments over the years as well, and I went to his graduation from the academy. Apparently, his promotion to Robbery-Homicide was so recent she hadn't yet had the chance to tell me about it. It was a bit of a mental disconnect to see him all grown-up and a cop no less, but I still occasionally saw hints of that thirteen-year-old in his smile.

Jesse and I started meeting for coffee a few times a week so he could catch me up on the latest news from the ongoing investigation, so we've been spending a lot of time together. I found myself looking forward to our meetings and not just because it was nice to see Jesse. The case was taking hold of me. I began to hunger for new information and the chance for us to bounce ideas off each other. I gained a new understanding of what keeps cops going during an investigation and how the idea of putting all the pieces together and solving the puzzle can become almost intoxicating. After viewing the photos of the first two victims, I was able to detach and tap into the clinical mindset that keeps those in my profession from becoming incurably depressed or losing all faith in humanity and hiding under our desks.

I was chatting with a grad student on the way back to my office when I caught sight of a familiar face. Holly, a woman I worked with at a record store more years ago than I'd like to count, was coming my way with a young man who looked to be around eighteen. I'd last seen her singing with a local band seven years ago, right before she moved to New York. She spotted me and smiled.

"Ashley! I was hoping we'd run into you!"

"Hi, Holly, it's so good to see you! You're a long way from home." She gave me a warm hug.

"I am, indeed. Do you remember my son, Damien? I was able to come out a week before the big label conference in LA, so we're touring colleges for a few days."

Holly had moved to New York to take a job with a large music distribution company and pursue her own artistic efforts. Damien and I shook hands and exchanged pleasantries. I avoided embarrassing him by pointing out that he was eleven years old the last time I'd seen him. One thing about not having children is that I don't have living, breathing reminders of how fast time is passing. Holly still looked much like she did when we worked together, but here she was with a grown man claiming to be her son.

"It's just not possible that you have a child this age," I said.

She smiled. "Believe me, it seems impossible to me too!"

We spent a few more minutes catching up and then made plans to meet for a drink that evening. I headed for my office thinking about the connections we make with people and how some fade over time yet some last forever. I have a few close friends from college, like Cait, and have made some particularly good friends among my academic colleagues. But I feel the strongest emotional connection with the people I worked with at Tower Records. Perhaps it has to do with the fact that we were all in our twenties and felt like we had our whole lives in front of us. We were paid—not very well—but somehow that didn't matter then to sell and listen to music. Even after I left the store for the corporate office across the river in West Sacramento to work in the advertising department, I was still surrounded by and immersed in music. It might also be that spending our formative years in such a diverse, tolerant, exciting atmosphere created a special bond. Whatever the case may be, my friends from those days will always feel like family.

6

As I left my office and walked out to the faculty parking lot, it started to rain, which is cause for celebration in California at this point. Five consecutive years of drought have taken their toll on the landscape, the water table, and our collective psyche. It had been a good one, but the final class of the day can go either way. Sometimes the students have already checked out, and I can't get anything resembling a discussion going. Other times, they're lively, animated, and really engaged. Fortunately, today it was the latter. It was shaping up to be a good semester based on the way my classes felt so far. Besides the pop culture course, Psychology of Personality has always been my favorite to teach, and it was a nice way to end the day. Psych 101 and Abnormal Psychology are prerequisites, so the students have a good basic foundation coming into the class. I was considering the subject of the first paper to assign when I reached my car and my phone chimed with an incoming text. It was Jesse, wondering if I could meet him at the station. That meant one of two things: either there was new evidence to share or a new crime had been committed. I shivered involuntarily and replied that depending on traffic, I'd be there in twenty minutes, give or take.

Detective Malone was quiet as we walked down the hallway to the conference room. I let him be, figuring he'd tell me why I was there soon enough. We sat down at the table, and under the harsh fluorescent lights, Jesse looked exhausted. He had dark circles under his eyes and apparently hadn't had time to shave that morning. A nice-looking Hispanic man in his fifties approached the glass doors and came into the room. Jesse introduced him as his partner.

"Ashley McKennitt, Detective Eduardo Marquez. Ed, this is Ash."

I stood and shook his hand. "Nice to meet you, Detective."

"Likewise, and you can call me Ed. So you're a psychology professor?"

"I am and I have the fancy diploma to prove it."

He smiled, creating a slight crinkling at the corners of his deep brown eyes.

"Jess, I just came in to meet the professor." He then looked back at me. "Sorry for the drive-by, but I have a meeting, so I'll leave you to it."

"No worries," I said. "Thanks for making the effort to come by and say hello."

He turned and left. Jesse watched him go, and I wondered how long he'd feel like the new guy in the department. Hopefully, the warmth I'd sensed in Detective Marquez made its way to Jesse. He grabbed a binder from the shelf behind him and said, "At five thirty this morning, a man was found in a room at the Economy Inn in North Sacramento. Cause of death was determined to be suffocation, pending the autopsy and a toxicology report. If this is the work of the same guy, and I think it is, we are dealing with one sick, twisted individual."

As he removed the photos of the scene and placed them in front of me, Jesse continued.

"According to the motel records, the man used the automated checkout on the television around 4:00 a.m. but then didn't leave. A maid working the early shift this morning used her pass key to get into the room she thought was empty and saw this…"

It took a moment for me to realize what I was looking at. A rather large man was lying on the unmade bed, fully dressed, including his shoes. His eyes were open, staring sightlessly at the ceiling. He was tied to the bed, not by his wrists and ankles but by heavy gauge rope wrapped around his body and the entire bed. The remote control was in his right hand. I looked at Jesse, speechless.

"Yeah, I know," he said.

"In the words of my students, dude, that is messed *up*."

Jesse read me the initial report taken at the scene. The forty-five-year-old White male was discovered by a maid at 5:35 a.m. The body showed no obvious signs of physical trauma. According to the man's driver's license, he lived in LA. His car was in the parking lot and hadn't been disturbed in any way. I looked back at the photo, feeling a vague sense of...what? Recognition? That couldn't be it. Why would anything in that photo look familiar to me? I'd never even been to the Economy Inn.

He must have seen something in my face.

"What is it?"

"Um, this is going to sound completely crazy, I mean totally insane," I said.

"That's why we call this brainstorming, Ashley. Any and all ideas are to be shared. Out with it."

I hesitated. "Okay, I think our guy is staging his crimes. He's creating these scenes for us to discover, and each one has a...a theme, for lack of a better word. It's like he's leaving us clues, and he can't wait for us to solve the riddle."

"Okay, so what's the clue here? What do you see?"

"Here's what's going to sound crazy. Do you know that Eagles song, 'Hotel California'? There's a line about being able to check out, but you can't leave."

Jesse stared at me. "That fits. And that's quite a calling card. Holy crap, what a sick bastard."

We sat in silence for a moment.

"So if we're dealing with the same guy here, if one person committed all three murders, do the other scenes relate to song lyrics too?"

"I don't know. Let's look at them again."

"Man, I need coffee for this. I'm going to see if there's any in the breakroom. Take a look at these in the meantime," he said, putting the other murder book and cold case file in front of me.

My mind was racing as fast as my pulse. I was very much aware that I might not only make a fool of myself with this outlandish theory but also make Jesse look bad, which would be quite detrimental to his career. No pressure there. I retrieved one photo each from the other two case files and studied them. If the killer was leaving clues having to do with popular music, he may not stick with a particular genre, but I assumed he would likely stay within a given era. Jesse returned and set a mug of coffee in front of me.

"I can't say it's fresh, but it's hot and strong."

"That'll work. Thanks."

He looked at the photos I was studying. "What do you think?"

I shook my head, pointing to the photo of the man in the park. "I don't know what to think. The paint-by-numbers thing is so freaking weird and random. And what's up with the letters? He deliberately painted A, B, C, D, E on the table in the guy's blood…oh!"

What?" Jesse asked.

"That Police song, 'Murder by Numbers.'" I started to hum it.

"I know that one," Jesse said. "Cait played that album all the time, but they count, don't they? It's by numbers, not letters."

I took my phone out of my purse and looked up the lyrics to make sure I was right.

"It didn't hit me until I said the letters aloud. They do sing one-two-three in the song but also mention the ABCs, and all five letters come at the end. I put my phone in front of Jesse.

"We're onto something here. What about the first one? If we can tie that murder to these two, I've got something to take to the captain."

I nodded. "The newspaper must be significant. Do you know if it was from the day the man died?"

Jesse looked through the file. "I don't know if that was noted. Why?"

I shrugged. "It might mean something if it was some other date."

I looked at the photo. Nothing came to mind, nada. This was nuts. I was suggesting to a homicide detective that a potential serial killer was leaving clues based on song lyrics at the scenes of his murders. I was starting to regret saying anything about my whacko theory.

"Sorry, Jesse, I've got nothing. Maybe we're going down the wrong path here."

"That's possible. I don't think we are and I think we need to keep at it, but I won't take this to the captain unless we're both convinced. Deal?"

I nodded. "Deal."

"Okay. So I dragged you down here right after work. I'm sure you have things to do and you're probably starving by now."

"I do have a little class work to do, and yeah, food isn't a bad idea. You weren't kidding when you said that coffee was strong."

He smiled and shrugged. "It's a cop thing."

He walked me out to the lobby where we said our goodbyes. I headed for the door, and then he said, "Ashley, wait. I really do think we're on to something. I know you doubt yourself, but I could tell you hundreds of stories about cases being solved because someone had the guts to float a much crazier-sounding idea than what you've come up with."

"Fair enough, Detective. We'll keep at it."

I walked out into the rain, heading for my car, and sincerely hoped he was right.

After a quick dinner, I made a cup of tea and sat on the couch with my class schedule and laptop. I'd laid out the general plan in the syllabus for each class, but there was still a bit of room for flexibility as far as the subject of papers and projects. I was contemplating subjects for the first paper in the personality class when I decided some music was in order. Can't go wrong with the Beatles on a rainy evening, or anytime, really. But which album? *Rubber Soul*? *Sgt. Pepper*? I went with the latter and settled down to work. After deciding on topics through the middle of the semester for the classes that required students to write papers, I returned some emails. By then, the last track of the album had begun. Holy crap. I grabbed my phone and called Jesse, who answered on the first ring.

"Hey, Ashley, what's up?"

"It's the Beatles, Jesse. The first victim, in the car. There's a line in the Beatles' 'A Day in the Life' about the guy blowing his mind out in a car."

"Oh my god, you're right. And isn't there something about the news that day?"

"Yeah, that's why the newspaper is significant."

"Good lord, this is huge. I need to write this up and go to the captain. What do you say, are we ready to do this?"

I took a deep breath. "Yeah, I guess. Hang on a minute, though, Jesse. I can't help but notice the differential in the risk levels here. My professional reputation isn't on the line like yours is."

"Let me worry about that."

"Are you sure?"

"Absolutely."

"Okay then, here we go…"

As worried as I was about Jesse potentially damaging his career, I felt in my gut that I was right. We were dealing with a cold, calculating psychopath who was creating sick riddles that he couldn't wait for the cops to try to solve. Then a deeply unsettling thought occurred. The riddles would have to get more intricate over time for our sicko to get the same buzz. That meant more horrendous crimes and more victims. My tea had gone cold by then, but that had nothing to do with the chill I suddenly felt.

7

As was the case most mornings, Jesse was at the café when I got there. He waved me over to our usual table, and I saw that he already had his coffee and had bought a latte for me.

"I'm pretty sure it was my turn," I said, gesturing at the cups.

"No worries, you can treat next time."

I thanked him and sat down.

"I got home late last night," he began, "so I didn't get a chance to tell you, but I caught up with Dr. Pereira yesterday."

"And?" I felt a little rush of nervous excitement. The good doctor and I were essentially professional colleagues with roughly the same amount of education. But her career path had taken her to the front lines, where she dealt with extremely troubled individuals and often saw the worst examples of human behavior, while I was safely removed from the fray. My biggest challenges were grading papers on time, keeping up with committee and research grant paperwork, and trying to keep students engaged and interested. I didn't know what her thoughts were on Jesse recruiting me to begin with, and I really had no idea what she'd make of what I'd come to think of as my left field theory.

Jesse smiled. "She told me up front that she thought it was a little unorthodox to go outside the department like I did without first looking at internal resources. But given her limited time in my precinct, she congratulated me on my resourcefulness."

That made me like her.

"I gave her a quick rundown of our working theory about who we're dealing with. She had actually just been reviewing the case files, so she was fully up to speed. Then I walked her through our thought process and how we arrived at the conclusion that our guy is setting the stage and creating riddles for us to solve. She was very intrigued and spent a few minutes explaining her involvement with a case several years ago in which the murderer left elaborate calling cards."

"What did she think about the riddles being song references?" I asked, bracing myself for an answer I didn't want to hear.

"She loved it. She's really impressed with your encyclopedic knowledge of music and said she'd like you to join her trivia team."

That made me like her quite a lot.

We spent a few more minutes talking about Dr. Pereira's thoughts on the case and where she thought the killer might go next, which led into what I wanted to talk to Jesse about. I'll admit that it was very validating to be on the same page as a police psychologist and feel like I was in the same league with her.

"What our guy might do next is what I wanted to talk to you about, Jesse. I think it's safe to say that we're dealing with a bona fide psychopath here. He's twisted but likely highly intelligent, possibly even a genius. He's deriving a lot of pleasure from planning his scenarios, which will likely get even more elaborate if this continues. But soon, he's going to tire of his own game. As with any drug, he's going to need more. He's going to want a bigger rush."

"And then what will he do?"

"This isn't what you want to hear, but it could be almost anything. He might have multiple victims, or maybe his riddles will become much more complex. He's literally getting away with murder, so he's winning, which is totally feeding his ego."

Jesse toyed with his empty coffee cup and then abruptly crushed it.

"You know that sense of detachment you talked about having to develop? I think I need a refresher course. I know I need to stay analytical about this. With determination and good detective work, we'll find him. But that bastard is out there right now, probably planning his next sick little play, and one—or more—of the citizens I'm sworn to protect is in danger."

Anyone who has lost faith in humanity or who thinks that good, honest, hardworking people don't exist anymore should have been sitting where I was. Jesse's drive to be a force of good in the face of malevolence was nothing short of inspiring.

"Do you remember what you told me the day you graduated from the academy?"

He shook his head.

"I asked why you wanted to be a police officer, and you said that you wanted to be one of the good guys."

A faint blush appeared on his cheeks. "I did? If I don't remember that, how do you?"

"It just now came back to me. You're right, you are going to find this guy. You and Ed will figure this out. He's outsmarting you and staying a step or two ahead for the time being. But he's not going to be able to sustain that because he's going to keep escalating his game."

"Does this guy want to get caught?"

"No. Not him. He's on a sick mission of some kind and thinks he needs to complete it. His riddles at the scene are his way of taunting you, of saying, 'See how much smarter I am? Bet you can't figure this one out.'"

"What are the chances of him slipping up and leaving a fingerprint somewhere?"

"Extremely slim, I'd say. Our sicko is very meticulous. Part of the rush is the elaborate planning that goes into his scenarios. He's not likely to make a careless mistake."

Jesse looked at his watch, picked up his crumpled coffee cup, and then tossed it into the trash bin across from our table. As we headed for the door, he said, "You have a lot of faith in me. I really appreciate that."

"Why wouldn't I? You're good at what you do. And speaking of faith, you brought an outsider into what could turn out to be one of the biggest cases of your career."

He shrugged. "Guess I'm just a rebel."

"A good guy rebel. I like it."

We rounded the corner of the building and were hit with an unseasonably chilly gust of wind. I'm not much for prophecy, but it felt like a sign of things to come.

8

Later that morning, I walked through the main quad, enjoying the crisp hint of fall in the air. It hadn't quite been cool enough yet, but over the next month, the trees would start to turn, and Mother Nature would treat us to a stunning display of her autumn palette. There was more activity than usual, and I realized the maintenance crew and organizers were starting to set up for the Fall Festival that takes place in late September. Local artisans display their handiwork, small businesses offer discounts on goods and services, and local media is represented by the weekly paper and a few of the radio and television stations in town.

"Hey, pretty lady, long time no see!"

I kept walking, assuming the comment was directed at someone else, when I recognized the voice. That annoyingly whiny, nasally voice. What the hell was he doing here?

"Ashley! Are you going to walk right by like you don't even see me?"

That was my plan.

"Lester. Hey. What are you doing here?"

"I came to help set up the booth. Can't leave everything to the interns, right? Hey, we've got to catch up. Let me buy you a cup of coffee."

"Sorry, but I'm on my way to class right now."

"Well then, how about a drink later this week?"

"I'll have to check my calendar..." Same old Lester. Still never gets a hint. And apparently still thinks he can pull off the latest fashion trends. Someone should tell him he's a bit long in the tooth to rock the skater boy look.

"So do that and call me," he said, tossing a business card at me.

Sure, Les, how about the tenth of never? I mumbled something incoherent and hurried off. Lester Burton is not someone I expect to run into these days. Back when I was going to school and working at Tower, I couldn't get away from the guy. He was new to radio sales then and showed up at the store at least once a week, trying to get me and the other buyers to give him endcaps and participate in his promotions. He finally figured out that he needed to go through the advertising department at the main office, which was great until I ended up there. Then he was always showing up with doughnuts or trying to get me to go to lunch with him and buy airtime I couldn't begin to get the record labels to pay for. If you look up *schmooze* in the dictionary, you'll find a picture of Lester.

I heard he'd done quite well for himself as of late. After trying to be a DJ, washing out as a band manager, launching an ill-fated record label, and lord knows what else, he'd gone back to sales and, given the booth he was currently setting up, had landed at the classic rock station in town. I was convinced his success was due to wearing people down. They agree to whatever he wants just to get him to *stop talking*. He has the gift of gab that makes him a natural for sales, but there's always been something slightly off about him. You just knew Lester was the kid who ate paste in grade school.

In an effort to continue to offer a robust curriculum and stay competitive within the state college system, the psychology department had recently expanded. The addition of three adjunct professors and two full-timers had indeed rounded out the course catalog but left the department chair with the dilemma of where to house the newcomers. The solution was to double up on offices, and those of us who'd inhabited the larger spaces began to share them. My office mate, Angelica Camryn, joined the department as one of the adjunct profs two years ago. This semester, she's teaching Clinical Psych and History and Systems of Psychology and is only on campus three days a week. She's just shy of six feet tall and has the big personality to match. She's bright, warm, incredibly outgoing, and has an infectious laugh. I could have done a lot worse for a roomie.

Due to Ang's part-time status and our staggered schedules, we aren't in the office at the same time all that much, making sharing the space pretty much a nonissue. Office hours on our shared days take place when the other is in class, giving our students the privacy to discuss whatever they might need to without having to worry about another professor in the room. Angelica is almost as much of a pop culture junkie as I am, so we generally spend most of our office time discussing music, what we're currently reading—apart from trade publications, textbooks, and student papers—and which movies we want to see. She followed through on her threat to sit in on my popular culture class this year, and not only is it fun to have her there but she's also adding a new dimension and a fresh perspective to the discussions.

*****

It was early, not quite light yet, and he was groggy from lack of sleep, but since the Other had come back, there hadn't been much time to rest. He'd been alone for quite a while, and then he felt it—his old friend was coming back for a visit. He'd prepared the welcome. And now it was time to plan another special event, this one more involved. It wouldn't do to be lazy and repeat something he'd already done. The Other would not be happy if he didn't try his absolute best with each offering. The first thing to do was select the subject. That was easy enough. There were plenty of people who had wronged him along the way, those who needed to be taught a lesson. Once that was decided, it would be time to go to work. He switched on the bedside lamp and consulted his list. So many choices. Ah yes …that one felt right. The Other would approve. He shuffled into the kitchen and made a cup of his special tea—the kind that opened the doors of perception—sat down at the table, and waited for the Other to ignite his imagination.

It was getting more difficult to plan an event while going about his daily business. His job brought him into contact with a lot of people, and some days it was almost impossible to listen to their yammering when he had so much work to do. But he had to keep up the pretense that he was one of them, a *normal*. As far as anyone knew, he was just another citizen, going about his job like all the other pathetic drones. Pretending to care about all the stupid things they got worked up about, like who was going to win the World Series or how much a gallon of gasoline cost. He had no time to think about such nonsense. There was only the success of the mission and pleasing the Other. After a morning spent mentally toying with different scenarios, he declined a lunch invitation, saying he needed to catch up on work. In truth, he couldn't eat in the early planning stages of an event. He needed to stay perfectly focused and plan every last detail. Only then could he let himself begin to feel the rush that would take hold of him and finally course through his body as he executed another perfect performance. The cops were such idiots. They still thought his events were unconnected and performed by completely different people. Morons.

That evening, he switched on the television to catch the news. His event was the top story on all three major networks. That would please the Other. The cops were referring to it as another isolated incident, the idiots. Staying several steps ahead of them was no sweat, child's play. He giggled. He switched to one of the cable news stations, the one that sensationalized everything, and sat down to watch. He'd get the most airtime there. The newscasters were practically salivating, saying they had exclusive footage and details no other station had. They were just dying to spill the juicy details, but the cops wouldn't let them. No, the media had to speak in general terms, dancing around the subject, lest a copycat try to stage his own event. As much as he'd like to hear about his handiwork on TV, it was best that the details were kept out of the news reports. It was unacceptable to think of a copycat stealing his thunder. That would not do.

Wait. What was this about an unnamed source helping the cops? He grabbed the remote and bumped up the volume. The airheaded blonde anchor was talking about the cops bringing in an outside expert as a consultant to offer insights into the criminal mind. The source was to remain anonymous for safety reasons, but the station had a tip that said expert was from the university. Well, isn't that interesting? Maybe some hotshot criminal justice professor who doesn't know shit about the real world is helping the cops and offering their BS "expertise." Pathetic. Still, it wouldn't be wise to get cocky. He'd need to check out this so-called expert to determine where they came from and whether they posed any real threat. Ah well, another piece to the puzzle just made it more intricate and would only add to the complexity of future events. It didn't matter who the cops brought on; he was unstoppable and smarter than all of them together.

9

A ngelica had already left for the day, so I locked up after my scheduled office hour. Stepping outside, I could see that we were in for another glorious autumn sunset. The sky changed and the colors grew deeper just during the short walk to my car. I pulled out of the faculty parking garage, joining the line of cars waiting to exit campus and turn onto J Street. I was headed downtown to meet friends for dinner and eager to talk to people who had nothing to do with university politics. Of course, I wouldn't be able to say anything about my involvement with an actual murder investigation, which was beginning to occupy my every waking thought. It had slowly dawned on me that as the investigation went on, it would be more difficult not to think about it, and Jesse and his partner would be the only ones I could talk to.

I parked down the block from the restaurant, and as I was walking toward it, a tall thin guy with a scraggly graying beard coming my way made eye contact. He looked vaguely familiar, but I couldn't place him. As we were about to pass each other, he said, "Don't I know you?"

His voice triggered my memory.

"Frank Jacobson?"

Wow. He looked completely different from the last time I saw him, which, granted, was more than twenty years ago. His expression didn't change as he said, "Oh hey…Ashley, right? I haven't seen you since you worked at Tower Records. What a trip to run into you after all this time."

"Hey, Frank, this is a surprise. I didn't know you were still in the area."

"I just moved back about six months ago. I was doing sound for a band called Scarecrow Incident, and after their last tour, I ended up back here."

We spent a few minutes catching up. Frank used to call on Tower when he worked for a record label. He wasn't very friendly back then, and I always thought he was a little odd, but he was good about getting us in-store events and making sure we had the new releases we needed. One of the other closing managers I worked with couldn't stand him and said she thought he was the guy most likely to snap and become an ax murderer. It was an extreme way of dismissing him as a creep, but looking back, there was something unsettling about his demeanor. He had a curious lack of affect that made him appear completely emotionally detached, and apparently that hadn't changed. I told Frank I was meeting friends, and we said our goodbyes.

I watched him walk away, wondering if that lack of emotion was a sign of something deeper…and more disturbing. Had my old colleague been more accurate than she knew? Then I chided myself for looking for demons around every corner. Frank may have been a little creepy, but did I seriously just wonder if he had extreme mental problems? If he was capable of hurting someone? How the hell can cops do their jobs without seeing everyone they encounter as a potential suspect? I walked into the restaurant, thinking about running into Holly, Lester, and then Frank. Guess it was old home week.

The next morning, I was on my way to the pop culture class, wondering what my students had in store for me—it was one of their days to bring in music they wanted to discuss—when I got a text from Cait asking if I had time to talk that evening. I replied that I absolutely did. It had been far too long since she and I had had one of our marathon phone conversations, and we were way behind with what was going on in each other's lives. I hadn't even known that she was back in the country. We agreed on seven thirty, and I walked into class smiling, which didn't last long once I discovered it was going to be gangster rap day. Not my favorite genre, but that choice always provides an excellent opportunity to talk about parental warning labels on music, more thoughts on censorship in general, and who gets to be the watchdogs that make those decisions.

After class, I had just enough time to check email and answer a few student inquiries before rushing across campus for a meeting. I'd been trying to at least appear to be more interested in what was going on in the psych department and the university in general since the department chair had chided me in my last review for my distain for campus politics. She'd told me she knew I didn't mean to come across as aloof, but that's how it appeared when I avoided all but absolutely mandatory meetings. Never one to mince words, she'd told me, "You'd do well to learn to play the game once in a while." At least she was honest.

That evening, I grabbed a large stack of mail on the way into the house, dodging Cody as he ran in circles around me. We went through our greeting ritual, and I let him herd me into the backyard to toss his ball. Anyone who's ever had a border collie knows that they will chase a tennis ball with a single-minded determination until they're completely exhausted. The scene with the dog and the ball in the movie *Dr. Doolittle* is not far from the truth. "Throw the damn ball!" And as much as Cody loves the activity and attention, it's good for me, too, to decompress from the day and transition from work mode, where I must be *on* all day, to being at home. Working at a small university means less stress in general, but I do still have to deal with department meetings, workshops, campus politics to an ever-increasing degree—thanks to my boss's recent admonition—and be available for my students.

The dog finally decided something on the other side of the fence was more interesting than the ball and ran over to investigate. I sat at my little patio bistro table and sorted through the mail, finding a letter from my friend in Washington, the usual junk, and way too many holiday catalogs, even though it was only September. It seems like every time I successfully remove my name from a mailing list, it ends up on three more. I put the letter on the table and gathered everything else to toss into the recycling bin, thinking about what a waste of time it obviously was to try and remove my name from any more lists.

Cody dashed over and sat down, tail thumping on the patio, looked at me, and then looked at the back door, which was his way of saying he wanted dinner. I'm convinced he thinks if he stares at me long enough, my little human brain will grasp what he's trying to tell me. I'm aware that anthropomorphizing is frowned upon, especially in my field, but I remain convinced that animals understand a lot more than much of the scientific community gives them credit for. Plus, border collies are known for being intelligent. Of course, some people might say I'm a typical pet parent who thinks my animal is brilliant. But hey, at least, I don't have a house full of cats I have long conversations with.

After reading student papers over dinner, I rinsed my dishes and put them in the dishwasher, made a cup of tea, and settled on the couch with my phone and a fleece lap blanket. It was probably cold enough in the house to turn on the heat, but I always try to make it as far into the year as possible—at least November—before I resort to that. For a woman who regularly bounces between time zones, Cait is remarkably prompt and called at exactly seven thirty. We got the usual "How are you?" and "It's been too long" preliminaries out of the way, and then she jumped into her reason for the call.

"Are you up for a house guest sometime soon? Like next week?"

"Of course! You know you're welcome here anytime. I'll be at work during the day, but we can hang out at night."

"That's perfect. I don't expect you to entertain me. I'd stay with my parents, but…"

"You don't need to explain. Besides, I'm going to very selfishly say that I want to monopolize as much of your time as I can."

"Aw…I miss you, my friend."

"Back atcha," I said. "So what have you been working on? I wasn't even sure that you were in the country."

She explained that she'd only been back in San Francisco for a few weeks, having spent the last two months in Northern Africa. She was ready to take a break and not think about her next assignment.

"Enough about me, though. I want to know what's going on with you and the investigation you're helping my brother with."

I had no idea how much, if anything, Jesse had shared with Cait. Decades-long friendship notwithstanding, I had to be careful of oversharing and accidentally spilling confidential information.

"Well, you know I can't say very much about it since it's an open investigation, but I'm offering a clinical perspective and helping to build a profile of the mystery suspect."

"Yeah, I get that, but can't you let one little detail slip? Like how many victims? Have they all been offed the same way?"

"Cait, come on. Those are not *little* details, and you know that's exactly the kind of stuff I can't talk about."

"Okay, you win—for now, but I had to try."

"Man, you journalists are unrelenting," I teased.

"Uh-huh, and you psychologists…"

"Careful how you finish that."

"Yes, Dr. Freud."

We chatted for another thirty minutes, about mutual friends, what we were doing for the holidays, and male company. I made a mental note to check my friend's band website. I thought Stephen had told me they were playing next weekend, but I wasn't sure. I wanted to bring Cait to a show not only because I knew she'd love the music but also because I wanted her to meet him. She promised to update me in person about the latest with Daniel, her on-again-off-again-repeat guy she's been seeing intermittently for at least three years, but it may be more by now. They can't seem to make it work when they're together, but they're miserable when they're apart. The conversation wound down, and we said our goodbyes. I let Cody out to do his business, and then we settled down for the night.

10

The next day, I had a full schedule, consisting of the usual office hours, research, and reading between classes. In addition to starting preliminary research on the paper I planned to write once the investigation wrapped up, I was working on validating the findings of one of my grad students who was in the process of piecing together her thesis. That would be an enjoyable but lengthy project. Working with post-grads has always been one of the most rewarding parts of teaching. I was lucky enough to have some excellent advisors when I was working on my advanced degrees, and mentoring my students felt like a nice way to pay that forward.

My morning office hour was nearly over when a freshman appeared in my doorway. An angry freshman.

"I need to talk to you about this grade, Professor," he said, waving an exam at me.

"Okay, come on in." I gestured at the chair in front of my desk.

"Kyle," he said, giving me plenty of attitude.

"I know your name, Kyle. What's the issue with the grade?"

"You gave me a D on this test." He tossed it on my desk.

"You earned a D. You answered 35 percent of the questions incorrectly. Multiple-choice exams are pretty straightforward."

"I need to take the test again."

"It doesn't work that way. But it's still early in the semester, and this is only one exam. You have plenty of time to bring your grade up."

"You don't understand. I've never gotten a D. I can't have this on my record."

I try to avoid sweeping generalizations about my students, but the young man in front of me was making it difficult not to pigeon-hole him as part of the entitlement generation who thinks everyone deserves a ribbon just for showing up.

"What I don't understand is why you're so upset about one grade on one test, Kyle. You certainly don't want this to be a trend, but one D isn't going to break your academic career."

He stared at me belligerently. Time to try a different approach.

"Look, the first semester at a university can be challenging. There's a lot to get used to, and you need to figure out how to manage your time. Maybe joining a study group—"

"I did study! This test is bogus."

So much for a new approach. I silently started to count to ten.

"Never mind," he said, standing up. "You're not even listening to me."

"Kyle, I am listening, and if you'd show me the same courtesy…"

He'd walked out without another word. I had to think there was more going on with him than a disappointing grade, but it was unlikely I'd find out, as he'd clearly decided I was the enemy. Unfortunately, every so often, I encounter a student I just can't reach.

Jesse sent a text midafternoon, asking me to come by the station that evening. He and Ed were working on a profile of the killer and wanted my input. That sounded much more appealing than looking at new crime scene photos. It also meant the killer had not yet stuck again, which was a nice—if not temporary—break. One of our biggest concerns was that the time between murders would decrease as the killer found more victims to feed his demons. There was a very real possibility that taking one life at a time wouldn't give him the high he craved, so he'd go after more. After leaving campus, I drove out to the station, checked in with the desk clerk, and waited for Jesse to come to the lobby.

Jesse had just finished reading the particulars of the autopsy report on the man found at the Economy Inn, which he thankfully didn't share with me, when he asked, "What's the clinical difference between a sociopath and a psychopath?"

"Psychologically speaking, we categorize both under the umbrella of antisocial personality disorders. They share a similar set of traits, primarily a poor inner sense of right and wrong. They can't seem to understand or share another person's feelings. A key difference is that while a sociopath has a conscience, it's weak. He may know that what he's doing is wrong, but he'll still do it. A psychopath not only lacks a conscience but is also unable to feel empathy. They're physically unable to respond to another person's distress. They can be quite intelligent, charming, good at mimicking emotions, and extremely manipulative, not to mention narcissistic. Some are very skilled actors whose sole mission is to manipulate people for personal gain. And while they're unable to feel remorse and typically don't feel fear, they can be paranoid and have an extremely low tolerance for frustration."

"But they can function in a regular job and be part of society? We're not talking about a creepy loner who lives in a shack by the river?" Ed asked.

"No, as much as we might like to think that. Our guy is out there right now, pretending to be a model citizen and masquerading as a productive member of society."

Jesse was quiet for a moment, flipping through the pages of a murder book, and then said, "We know little about him physically, though he's likely not a very big guy. Given the angle of trajectory of the bullet in the first case, the killer had to have been in the back seat. Since it was a two-door Toyota, there's not a lot of room back there."

"True, but if he's not that big, how did he overpower his other victims? A gun, even if he didn't use it?" I said.

"Perhaps. Of course, crazy is damned scary," Jesse answered.

"Good point."

"He's also most likely right-handed," Ed stated, "given the location of the bullet wound and the way the man in the park had his throat cut."

"That's not much to go on," I said.

Jesse agreed and went on to say, "Ashley, what do you think about speaking with Dr. Pereira? You haven't been able to talk to anyone but Ed and me about this investigation, and no matter how interesting it is to you from a clinical perspective, you're dealing with murder—actual dead people—for the first time."

"That's a good idea. I knew intellectually that getting involved in the investigation would affect me, but I hadn't really thought about how not being able to discuss it with anyone I know would feel."

He handed me her business card and said, "Give her a call. She's busy, but she'll make time for you."

"Thanks. Um…"

"What?"

I was a little hesitant to share what I wanted to say in front of Ed, whom I was still getting to know.

"Just something kind of weird that happened the other night. I ran into a guy I used to work with at the record store. He was a little creepy back then and hasn't changed much. I walked away, wondering if he could be our killer. Does that happen to you guys? Do you look at everyone as a potential suspect?"

"No. Just the weirdos," said Jesse.

I gave him a sarcastic grin, and Ed rolled his eyes.

"In all seriousness," Jesse began, "becoming a cop absolutely changes the way you look at the world. That's why the burnout rate is so high. But if you believe strongly enough in your ability to make a difference, you will."

"Said one of the good guys."

He smiled. "That's right."

Ed leafed through a report compiled by one of the junior officers who had canvassed the area around the motel, looking for anyone who might have heard or seen anything odd around the time the man died. "Nobody saw anything, nobody heard anything, just like with the man in the park. This guy is a goddamned phantom."

"Aren't eyewitness accounts a little iffy in a lot of cases?" I asked.

"They often turn out to be, but for every eighty to one hundred that are useless, there's one that gets us somewhere," Ed answered.

"Wow, those odds are inspiring."

"Welcome to our world, Professor," said Jesse.

A world in which the good guys plug away despite the odds. We paged through the murder books, reread reports, and bounced ideas around for another hour before calling it a night.

11

Cait and I were in the kitchen attempting to recreate a vegetable curry she'd had in Morocco she was sure I'd love when Jesse arrived. She rinsed her hands and ran to the door, towel in hand, trailing Cody, who'd bolted when he heard the doorbell.

"Hey, little brother!"

Jesse hugged her, lifting her feet off the floor. "Hey, sis, good to see you!"

Seeing the two of them together was almost surreal; they look more alike than most twins I know, sharing the same deep blue eyes and café latte skin tone. Cody barked, ran in circles, and sniffed Jesse's shoes, which is pretty much what anyone coming to my house can expect. I let him complete his ritual, then put my index finger on the bridge of my nose, and said, "Look." Once I had his attention, I gave the command to sit, and he complied. Border collies have a reputation for being easy to train, which is true if you go about it properly. They're very energetic, and some are strong-willed, but they're also quite intelligent, and if you're diligent about training when you're bonding with the dog, consistent with the commands, and establish a routine so they know what to expect, you'll end up with a well-behaved animal.

Jesse seemed a little unsure of how to greet me. I hadn't thought of it being particularly awkward, but here he was in my home as a guest rather than a professional colleague. He finally decided on the sideways half hug, putting his arm around me with his hand on my shoulder. Cait was already back in the kitchen, checking on her creation, and, from there, called, "What are you drinking, bro? Want a beer?"

"Sure," he answered.

She'd picked up a six-pack of his favorite when we were at the grocery store earlier. Good thing, too, since I know nothing about beer. We went to join her, Cody's nails ticking on the hardwood floor and Jesse asking about the house and how long I'd been there. I had a hunch he was wondering how much college professors make.

"I was lucky. The timing was right, and I was able to buy it about six months before the market went nuts. Now there's no way I could ever afford this neighborhood."

He nodded. "The same thing is starting to happen in my area but not as drastic. I keep thinking I should make some upgrades, but then I get nervous about spending the equity and getting stuck if the market tanks."

"It's a gamble, for sure, and no one has a crystal ball."

"Right. Remember being told how great it is to own a house?"

I nodded. "Yeah. Yet more proof that growing up is a trap."

"I'll drink to that," he said, touching his beer bottle to my wine glass.

Cody was sitting at Jesse's feet, looking up at him as though he expected a treat. Jesse patted his head and asked how long I'd had him. I told the story of going through border collie rescue and how it was love at first sight for both of us.

"What's border collie rescue?"

"One of the many breed-specific adoption agencies that make it easy to find the kind of dog you're looking for. Sometimes they have puppies available, but for the most part, they're older dogs that have been surrendered and need permanent homes."

Jesse looked confused. "I know people do that with pit bulls, but who would give up a dog like this guy?"

"You'd be surprised. A lot of people think they want a border collie because they've heard how smart they are, so they assume they're easy to train, which isn't necessarily true if you're not willing to make the commitment. But the most common reason for surrender is that the dogs are far more energetic than people expect and need a lot of stimulation, or they get bored. That can lead to destructive behavior, like eating window blinds, which is apparently what this guy did," I said, patting Cody's side. "I don't understand why anyone would get a dog if they didn't want to walk it and give it a lot of attention, but people have odd ideas."

"You lucked out, buddy," Jesse said, scratching Cody's ears. I sensed a bromance brewing.

When dinner was ready, we sat down at the dining room table, which I realized I hadn't used much lately. I enjoy entertaining, so why had it been so long since I'd had friends over? That was sure to change with the approaching holidays, but I thought about making a conscious effort to invite people over more often going into the New Year. Cait was right about her Marrakesh curry; we served it over couscous, and it was fabulous. We chatted about Cait's travels, her latest projects, and Jesse's recent promotion into Robbery-Homicide. Cait hadn't seen him since he'd made the jump in rank. I was wondering if she was going to press him on the details of the investigation like she did me when she said, "So, Jess, what's it like to be working such a high-profile case so quickly out of the gate?"

"Exhilarating, terrifying, and maddening all at once," he answered.

"Do you know yet if the murders are connected? Are you thinking serial killer?"

Jesse paused with his fork in the air. "What? You know I can't tell you that."

"Oh, come on, I'm asking as your sister, not a journalist."

"It doesn't make any difference. I still can't discuss any details with you. And given what you do for a living, you should know what the rules are."

She sighed. "I am well aware of the *rules*, but there's a big story here, and I want it. How about letting me know the locations where the bodies were found so I can check them out?"

"Seriously, Cait? Are you trying to get me fired?"

"Don't be so dramatic," she said, rolling her eyes. "I'm not asking you to let me photograph actual crime scenes or anything. I just want to document where the murders have taken place. That's public knowledge, isn't it? It's been on the news, and these *are* public locations we're talking about. Come on, man, give me something."

Jesse took a sip of beer, gently set the bottle down, and said, "Look, I know you're very good at what you do, and I get it that you want in on a high-profile story like this. But it's murder, Cait, dead bodies. Besides the fact that I cannot discuss an ongoing investigation—with *anyone*—I really don't want you to have anything to do with this. You'll have to forgive me if I don't want my only sister digging into a multiple homicide."

"Well, only brother, do I have to remind you that I've been to Iraq and Afghanistan? That I've seen war-torn cities and been in the middle of widespread destruction?"

"No, you don't. But can you blame me for wanting to forget?"

"You know, you're really annoying when you act like this. I don't need to be protected."

"I'm annoying? You are so freakin' hardheaded sometimes—"

"You don't earn a Pulitzer by being meek."

"I'm not questioning your qualifications or your drive," Jesse said, "but I'm allowed to worry. Sue me for caring."

Cait stared at him and then smiled, looking for a moment like the nineteen-year-old I met in the dorms so many years ago. "Okay, you win...for now."

I was relieved to feel the tension melt away. As close as they are, Cait and Jesse can both be hotheaded, and neither ever wants to be the first to back down. I hate being around that kind of unease, especially among friends; it's a middle child thing. We don't like conflict. And yes, I know what that says about my psyche and my choice of career. After dinner, Jesse insisted on helping with the dishes while Cait made coffee. I then served homemade apple crisp, the product of a trip to Apple Hill the previous weekend. We ate in the living room with the Beatles as background music. Who can be tense while listening to the Beatles? Cody gazed adoringly at Jesse and then settled at his feet with a sigh. Traitor.

Cait joined Cody and me on our run through McKinley the next morning. I was surprised she didn't want to sleep in, given how busy she'd been, but Cait has never been one to slack. No one could accuse me of being lazy, but her activity level puts mine to shame. I've always thought it has a lot to do with her career choice and her love of jumping onto a plane at a moment's notice without knowing when she'd return. She gets antsy if she's in one place too long. In stark contrast, I tend to be a homebody. I've never been sure if our enduring friendship is a case of opposites attracting or something else entirely, but I can't begin to imagine my life without her.

We completed our circuit of the park and slowed to a walk to cool down for the last block. We'd just turned the corner onto my street when Cait said, "So I promised you an update on Daniel…"

"You did. What's the latest? Are you two seeing each other again?"

"No. Well, not romantically. But we've gotten together for drinks a few times and have been talking quite a bit lately. He's been aggressively going after some high-roller clients and is going to be traveling more often. I think he likes bouncing things off me because I have nothing to do with his industry."

"That makes sense. And romantically involved or not, you're always there for him."

"Yeah…not sure if that's always a good thing," she said.

Daniel MacMillan is one of those go-getter types who never rests, which was one of the reasons he interested Cait in the first place. He's educated, articulate, and quite handsome, which didn't hurt. Daniel owns and operates a company called Your Dream Ride out of San Francisco. He's a classic and luxury car broker, who travels the world to put clients into the cars of their dreams.

"Good thing or not, you two are connected," I said, unlocking the front door and letting us into the house. "That's nothing to scoff at." Cody herded me into the kitchen, and I poured kibble into his bowl.

"I know and I do appreciate whatever it is that keeps us connected even when we're not together. It would just be nice to be normal and boring occasionally."

"Since when have you ever settled for normal and boring?"

"Touché," she said with a grin.

"I need to shower and get to work. Help yourself to whatever looks good for breakfast."

"Think I'll make a smoothie. You want one?"

"Absolutely, thanks." Cait's smoothies are incredible. I headed down the hall thinking that I could get used to someone making me breakfast.

I'd made an appointment to meet with Dr. Pereira after lunch, before my personality theory class. She invited me into her office and greeted me with a warm smile and a firm handshake. She had the graceful posture of a dancer and wore her chestnut-brown hair in a short, stylish cut. Aware that I was admiring her outfit, a teal silk blazer and impeccably tailored gray slacks, she said, "I splurge on something luxurious a few times a year. Clothing is the one indulgence I'll allow myself."

"You have great taste. That jacket is beautiful," I said, wondering what she thought of my minimal fashion sense, which involves jeans whenever possible. We sat down and chatted briefly about our similar educational backgrounds, and then she got down to business.

"I know I don't need to tell you, Ashley, how important it is to have someone to talk to about the investigation."

"No, you don't. I was actually going to ask Jesse about the possibility of speaking with you, but he suggested it first."

"He has good intuition. I'm a little concerned about his dealing with a case of this magnitude since he's new to Robbery-Homicide, but we're not here to talk about him. How are you dealing with the investigation?"

"As well as can be expected, I guess," I said. "I mean there was no way we could have known how involved it was going to get, that there would be another murder and...possibly more."

"Do you regret getting involved?"

"At times, and I've said that to Jesse. When I first agreed to get involved, he asked me to promise I'd tell him if I wanted out, which I don't. Mostly, I can maintain my clinical sense of detachment and focus on trying to figure out what's going on in that twisted mind. Plus, the thought of helping to get an extremely dangerous person off the street is not something most of us ever have a chance to do."

"But," she prompted.

"But it's becoming more difficult not to think about it. The investigation has really taken hold of me and is nearly always on my mind. It sounds a little melodramatic to say this, but it's changing the way I look at everything."

I told her about running into Frank downtown and walking away, wondering if he could kill someone.

"You're dealing with murder in an up-close-and-personal way plus viewing crime scene photos for the first time. That's going to change your outlook."

I nodded. Even though Jesse said she was on board with my pop culture-fueled theory, sitting there in front of Dr. Pereira, I was nervous about bringing it up. I took a deep breath and slowly let it out.

"So Jesse said he shared my left field theory with you. Do you really think we're on the right track?"

"I have to admit I was a little taken aback at first," she began. "But not only do you have the benefit of an outside perspective, your publishing history and credentials are impressive. I looked you up after Jesse brought you in," she said with a smile. "I'm convinced that this individual is taunting us as you've suggested, and if his psychosis presents as I think it does, he would be the type to leave a calling card and take great pleasure in setting up his gruesome scenarios."

"Do you agree that he's going to need to escalate to get the same rush?"

She nodded. "Unfortunately, yes. That's exactly what I think."

Great. That was something I'd love to be wrong about.

"Can I ask how long you've been doing this? And have you always been in the criminal justice realm?"

"For almost fifteen years. Early on, I flirted with the idea of going to med school and being a psychiatrist, but I just couldn't see taking on that level of student debt unless I was really driven to go that route, which I decided I wasn't. So I changed course and headed down the CJ path. I guess I've just always wanted to help the good guys."

I smiled. She and Jesse had common ground they didn't even know about.

"So how do you maintain your detachment? How do you keep from taking it home with you?"

"I drink a lot," she deadpanned.

I gave her a small laugh.

"In all seriousness," she began, "that was something I had to work on. And I keep working on it—it's like exercising, you must keep doing it. I think most of us go into this field because we want to help people, so we're empathetic. Turning that off when things get too intense seems counterintuitive at first."

"It does. How can you help if you're trying to distance yourself?"

"Exactly. But as we learn firsthand about the kind of pain and suffering that far too many people are experiencing, if we don't build up some emotional armor and learn how to take that step back, we'll never make it. Then we help no one, including ourselves."

"I had a similar discussion with a grad student the other day. She wants to go into counseling at-risk children but is starting to wonder if she'll be able to handle it."

"What did you tell her?"

"We talked about building up that armor and not losing sight of self-care. But I also told her there will be times when she'll doubt her ability to get through the day and will have to dig deep for the drive to help."

She cocked her head. "What was her response?"

"She thanked me for being honest and not blowing smoke at her."

"Nicely done, Professor."

I glanced at the clock and saw that I had about twenty minutes before I had to head back to campus. Dr. Pereira, who by then had insisted I call her Colleen, and I chatted a bit about grad school and where we thought we were headed in those days. She then asked me what I liked most about teaching.

"There are a lot of things. I especially like working with grad students and hearing about their plans for the future. I also enjoy the class discussions in my personality and contemporary issues classes. Once the students get comfortable with me and each other, hearing their world views and their sense of excitement at realizing they can potentially make a difference in people's lives is something I'll never get tired of."

She smiled. "That sounds pretty rewarding. I know you have to leave soon, but I wanted to talk about your pop culture class. First, how fun, and second, how did that come about?"

"It's tremendous fun and has become even more in demand than I'd hoped. As for how it happened, I was incredibly lucky. One of my all-time favorite profs was my adviser when I was completing my master's. He continued to mentor me once I went to Berkeley to work on my doctorate, which is where I presented the paper I adapted and use as a text for the class. Professor Lucas is now on the board at Sac State, and when I submitted the proposal to have the course added to the catalog, he was my champion, I think largely due to his having been such a fan of Tower Records for many years."

She smiled. "I'll bet it had a lot to do with you personally too."

I thanked her and said I needed to get going. She walked me out to the parking lot to take what she called a sky break. We exchanged numbers, and she asked that I promise to keep in touch.

"I'll pester you if you don't, and I was serious when I told Detective Malone I'd like you on my trivia team—you'll be our secret weapon."

"That sounds fun. Count me in."

"Excellent. Have a good rest of the day and we'll talk soon."

"We will," I said and headed for my car.

I'd cancelled my office hour that afternoon so I could meet with Dr. Pereira and got back to campus about an hour before the personality theory class. When I walked into my office, I found a plain brown cardboard box on my desk. It was about the size of a shoebox and bore a computer-generated label with my name and the address of the university, but there was no return address. According to the postmark, it was mailed locally. I asked Angelica if she knew where it came from.

"It was sitting there when I came in," she said, getting up and coming over to my desk.

"Are you going to open it?"

I hesitated briefly and then decided I was being paranoid. One of these days, I'll learn to listen to my gut. I sliced through the tape that sealed the box with a letter opener and pulled back a flap, and Angelica let out a shriek. I quickly closed the flap and shoved the box to the edge of my desk. Someone had sent me a dead rat.

"Oh my god!" Angelica said. "What a horrible stunt. Who would do that?"

Good question. A disgruntled student? Would Kyle do something like this? Or—no, I wouldn't let my brain go there. At the risk of his thinking I was overreacting, I called Jesse and filled him in. He took it quite seriously.

"Call campus security and report it. Don't touch the box again or tell anyone else about it. I'm on my way."

When the security operator picked up, I anticipated having to go into detail about my special delivery. He simply said, "Oh yeah?" and told me he was sending someone over. Perhaps receiving a dead rodent wasn't such a rare occurrence on campus. There was a cheerful thought.

When Jesse arrived, I introduced him to Angelica as a friend who happens to work for the police department. I hadn't yet said anything to her about my being involved with the investigation. Fortunately, she was too freaked out about the rat to ask why I'd called a cop instead of just letting campus security deal with it. The security guard, Matt, finished filling out his report and reached for the box, but Jesse stopped him.

"You can just leave that here."

"You sure? You don't want me to get rid of it for you?"

"No thanks, we've got it."

Matt shrugged, said, "Suit yourselves," and then left.

"I'll take this to the lab to see if they can get any prints off the box or the label. Maybe they can even figure out where the rat came from."

"How would they do that?" Angelica asked.

"Rats will eat just about anything. There might be a clue in the contents of its stomach."

"Oh," she said, looking as though she were deeply sorry for asking.

I wasn't yet ready to believe it had come from the killer.

"Jesse, this could just be a student prank, or someone upset over a final grade last semester."

"Are you having problems with any students right now?"

"There's one who was pretty upset over a poor test grade."

"Did you teach summer school?"

"One class."

"Did you fail anyone?"

"Well, no, but…"

"Look, I'm going to go by the book here and treat this as a threat. At the very least, it's harassment, but we need to accept the possibility that it came from…from someone other than a student," he said, glancing at Angelica. "If it turns out to be a harmless but sick prank—which is what I'd prefer, by the way—you'll get to say, 'Told you so.'"

I nodded, feeling a cold, prickly fear creep into my stomach. It was slowly sinking in that I was quite possibly no longer anonymous to the killer. In the blink of an eye, the game had changed. I decided not to share this latest development with his sister, which I was sure would make Jesse happy.

12

Saturday morning, Cait and I walked a few blocks to a nearby café, leaving Cody at home, much to his dismay. I see plenty of people do it, but I think it's cruel to leave a dog tied outside a restaurant while his owners eat. Besides, I planned to make it up to him tomorrow when I took Cait on one of my favorite hikes in Auburn, off Highway 49. Walking into the café, I watched people—especially men—turn to look at Cait. It was disarming at times during our college years, but I've grown used to people noticing, if not openly staring, at Cait wherever we go. The product of a blue-eyed Irish American father and an exotically beautiful mother from Barbados, she is downright stunning. And with her engaging, dynamic personality, people are naturally drawn to her.

We placed our orders and then snagged a table as a couple with a toddler left. We sat down, and she said, "I talked to Daniel this morning."

"And?"

She sighed. "Something seems...I don't know, just off."

"What do you mean?"

"He's getting ready to go to Germany to see some private Porsche collection, but he doesn't have a buyer."

"That's not so weird, is it? Doesn't he often scope out collections?"

"Yeah, but it's a bit odd that he'd go all the way to Europe without at least a potential prospect. And this is a last-minute trip, so it's not cheap."

"Maybe there are some real gems to be had."

"Maybe. He just sounded really distracted and not himself. I kept asking if he wanted to pick up our conversation later, and he said no but was barely paying attention."

About twenty minutes later, the waitress brought our food and utensils, asking if we needed anything else. We declined and spent a few minutes savoring our breakfasts. Cait opted for French toast with a side of scrambled eggs, and I had a Belgian waffle with strawberries, figuring I'd burn off the carbs on tomorrow's hike. In truth, I've never met a waffle I didn't like and would eat them every weekend if I didn't try to curb that craving. That's what I get for being half Belgian.

"Daniel is pretty driven, like someone else I know," I said. "He was probably just thinking about the cars and focused on what he needs to do before his trip. It's no big deal to you, but most of us don't jet off to another country at a moment's notice."

She shrugged. "I guess that's true. Most of his traveling has been within the US lately, and going to Germany to see some Porsches could be a pretty big deal."

"Right? What part of Germany?"

"Some remote village in the North Black Forest."

"Well, there you go. He's thinking about some eccentric dude in a tiny little village and pristine cars with hardly any miles on them."

She gave me a tiny smile and nodded in agreement, but she was obviously still concerned about Daniel. I let it go for the time being, knowing Cait would come back to it when she had more information or talked to him again.

"Oh, he wanted me to tell you that he found the perfect car for you."

"Oh yeah? My dream car?"

She smiled. "It's a 2010 Mustang Shelby 500GT. Cobalt blue with white stripes."

"Seriously? A Shelby? Has he forgotten that I'm a college professor?"

"He'd be sure you got a good deal."

"That would have to be one hell of a deal. A 2010 would still be around forty grand."

"You know he'd do his best for you. Besides, classic notwith-standing, don't you wish you had something newer?"

I shrugged. "Sometimes, but I'm not going to take on a mountain of debt to get there."

"Understood. Just keep it in mind."

It would be nice to drive something of this century and not have to worry about costly breakdowns. But a Shelby? I thought Daniel had been hanging out with the elite for too long. We ate the rest of our breakfasts and chatted about nothing of consequence, enjoying the comfort of our long-standing friendship.

Following a quiet evening, we woke up to one of those perfect October mornings that held the promise of a beautiful day. There was a crisp taste of autumn in the air, and the sky was deep blue. Cody recognized the signs of my preparing for a hike and, after running around in circles, went to sit by the front door. I was filling water bottles while Cait put on sunscreen.

"How does he know he's going with us?" she asked.

"The backpacks, my boots…I told you how smart he is."

"Yeah, but come on. You're saying he really knows what those things mean?"

I shrugged. "You saw his reaction when I took the packs out of the hall closet. He really does pay attention to things like that, but he's also heard us talking about going hiking."

At the mention of that word, Cody came back into the kitchen and tried to herd me toward the front door.

"Hang on, buddy. We're almost ready."

Cait shook her head. "I wouldn't have believed that unless I'd seen it. So what I've read about border collies being able to understand as many words as a toddler is true?"

"It is. Supposedly some are on par with the average five-year-old."

"Remind me not to tell any secrets in front of your dog."

Ten minutes later, I pulled onto Highway 80 at J Street and headed east. I wanted to take Cait to Auburn, about thirty-five miles away, where there are several hiking trails around the confluence, the point at which the north and middle forks of the American River come together. Traffic was light for a Sunday morning, it being too early in the year to see skiers and snowboarders heading for Tahoe. Of course, if the drought continued, they'd have no reason to make the trek. We kept the conversation light, which was fine with me. I wanted to enjoy the day and forget about psychotic serial killers and whatever Daniel was dealing with. Cait seemed to be in a similar frame of mind, talking about how long it had been since she'd been this far east on Highway 80 and how quickly the landscape changes after leaving Roseville.

"Do you get the feeling you're not in The City anymore, Dorothy?"

She laughed and reached back to pet Cody. "This beats the hell out of Oz, right, Toto?"

I took the Elm Avenue exit to Highway 49 south and headed down toward the river. That part of the road is extremely steep and winding, which seemed to take Cait by surprise.

"Good lord, I'm glad you're driving."

"Um…you live in San Francisco. You have hills that are way steeper than this."

"Yeah, but ours are straight up and down, with the exception of Lombard, of course, which natives avoid."

We rounded a corner, and the river came into view. Cody started whining with anticipation, and Cait said, "No kidding, Cody, what a view!"

Quite a few cars were parked along the highway and in the lot that connected to the access road, which led to the Quarry Trail, so named for the limestone quarry that was in operation during the gold rush. I paid the fee and pulled into a spot. Cait, who's used to paying exorbitant prices for parking in the Bay Area, was appalled that the people who parked along the road did so to avoid paying.

"Doesn't the money go to the Parks Department?"

"It does. You'd think these guys would want to support the agency that takes care of their playground."

"If only the rest of the world were as logical and levelheaded as we are."

"Right?"

I let Cody out of the car and told him to heel. He wanted to bolt for the trailhead but knew we had to get out of the parking lot first. He truly is an amazingly well-behaved dog. We started down the access road, and then I told him he was free. He took off running, the picture of pure joy, and then raced back and circled us.

"Aren't you worried about him taking off?" Cait asked.

"No. I invested in a good training course. It wasn't cheap, but I learned a lot, and it really did pay off. Not only is he very well trained but now we're also bonded—we are pack."

I had his leash in my backpack just in case we encountered a lot of other dogs, but I could trust that he'd trot alongside us without it.

The Quarry Trail follows the middle fork of the American River, eventually running into the Western States Trail in Cool if you're inclined to go that far. It's not a difficult hike by any means, but we planned to take our time and meander, taking breaks when we wanted and turning around to head back when we'd had enough. We hiked for an hour or so, enjoying the scenery, the clean air, and the quiet.

"My editor called last night with a lead on what could be a huge story," Cait said.

"Oh yeah, what kind of story?"

"Racketeering and a shady casino owner who's involved with drugs, prostitution, and money laundering. You know, your standard Vegas bad guy stuff."

"Holy crap, that is huge, but isn't it a bit out of your realm?"

"It is, but it's also way too big to stand by and watch someone else pick up and run with."

"I get that. So what exactly is racketeering? That's one of those terms you hear, but I have no idea what it actually means."

She paused to take a sip of water. "To be honest, I wasn't sure either. Basically, it's a criminal act where someone offers a service to solve a problem that wouldn't exist without the racket—a planned or organized criminal act. A classic example is the frightened business owner paying a protection fee to the bad guys so they leave him alone and let him stay in business."

"Oh, that's actually pretty simple."

"Right? Anyway, I'm taking off for Vegas in the morning."

"Okay." I was used to Cait coming and going as she chased a story. "But do you really have to go to Vegas? If this guy is into…all of that, are you sure you want to be poking around on his turf?"

She sighed. "You're starting to sound like my brother. Look, I'm just going to do some preliminary investigating to see if there's really a story there."

"Okay, fair enough." I wasn't really okay with it but couldn't very well lecture her about putting herself in harm's way when I was entrenched in a murder investigation.

We spotted a large, flat rock at the river's edge and stopped for water and granola bars. I removed a collapsible silicon bowl from my backpack, expanded it, and filled it with water. Cody waited patiently for me to set it down.

"Whoever came up with that is a genius," Cait said.

"Yes. Yet another of the many 'Why didn't I think of that?' things I've found since adopting this guy. I've learned to be careful— my wallet was taking a hit every time I bought dog food."

There's something inherently calming about being near water. Sitting there in the autumn sunshine with my two best friends, watching the river flow by, made me feel like I was a million miles away from the ugliness that was continuing to unfold in the city I called my home.

13

The next day, I was in my office grading Psych 101 exams when Ryan, a grad student, stopped by. He's one of those quiet, sincere kids who make me defend his generation when my colleagues start to denounce millennials.

"Hey, Professor McKennitt, do you have a minute?"

"Sure, Ryan, come on in. What's going on?"

He sat down across from me and said, "I wanted to talk to you about, um…"

I let him gather his thoughts rather than pressing him, which I'd learned was the best way to handle the quieter students.

"How did you know that psych was the right field for you?"

Ah. As happens to many post-graduate students, it seemed that Ryan was doubting his choice of majors, most likely due to thinking about his immediate job opportunities once he was out of school.

"I didn't at first. In fact, I didn't declare it as my major until my junior year. But no matter how many classes I took or other disciplines I explored, I kept coming back to psych because nothing else interested me as much."

He was silent for a moment, letting that sink in.

"Are you thinking you might want to go in a different direction?" I asked.

"No, it's not that. I've just been wondering if I really have what it takes to be a good counselor."

"I certainly think you do. You're empathetic, intuitive, and an exceptionally good listener."

He smiled. "Thanks. But what I mean is…lately I've been wondering if I'll be able to maintain that emotional distance, the sense of detachment you talk about. How do you shut off your emotions when you're trying to help someone?"

"That, Ryan, is a question we all ask ourselves at one point or another. I was heading down the clinical research path when I got my first teaching gig and decided this is what I wanted to be doing. I figured out early on that I'm someone who would have to work extremely hard at keeping that emotional distance. I knew it would continue to be a struggle for me. With a teaching gig, not only do I get to enjoy talking about what interests me in this field and work with you grad students, but I'm removed from the fray. I don't have to worry about maintaining that distance to keep myself in a place where I can be of help." Until I'm involved in a murder investigation, of course.

He nodded. "That makes teaching sound pretty good. So you know how I'm interested in substance abuse…it seems like that might be one of the more difficult places to keep that distance."

"You're right, it is. I'm not going to sugarcoat it. If you go that route, you'll see people at their worst, families torn apart, and lives thrown away. But you'll also have an opportunity to make a real difference for some people who can't get out from under on their own. And don't forget, with your education, you're going to have options. You don't have to decide right this minute what you're going to do for the rest of your life."

He smiled. "Yeah, I guess I don't."

"I'm going to check with a colleague to see if she might have some time to chat with you. I'll pass on her contact info if she does." It occurred to me that Colleen Pereira might be able to give Ryan a different perspective than I could offer.

"Thanks, Professor McKennitt. For what it's worth, I'm glad you ended up teaching."

"That's worth quite a lot, Ryan, thank you."

Moments like that made me sure I was in the right place, doing what I was meant to be doing.

I finished grading papers a little past noon and headed for the faculty dining room to find something edible for lunch. I spotted a few colleagues I could sit and eat with but just didn't feel up to the same conversations about my department and idle campus gossip. How could I pretend to be interested in who was upset over not getting a grant or who was going to retire next when the murder investigation I was supposedly helping with was going nowhere? The department chair's advice to learn to play the game echoed in my head, but I just couldn't make myself sit down at a table. Instead, I took my to-go salad and went outside. Surely Lydia couldn't fault me for wanting to enjoy the perfect autumn weather.

I found a bench where I could sit with my back to the sun and watched students coming and going, squirrels foraging, and professors hurrying between buildings. All occurring on a beautiful day under a bright blue sky. The same sky under which an extremely disturbed individual was no doubt plotting his next gruesome riddle for Jesse and Ed to discover. A riddle I was supposed to help solve. I thought about the dead rat I'd recently received. If it wasn't from Kyle or another disgruntled student, which I honestly didn't think it was, that left coming to terms with the fact that the killer knew where I worked. What was to stop him from coming to campus? He could easily blend in with students and faculty, wandering between buildings and scoping out Amador Hall.

It was obviously easy to discover where I work, so how difficult would it be to find out where I live? How the hell did I get to this point? I was a college professor at a state university, going about my nondescript suburban life. Things like this didn't happen to me or to anyone I knew. In offering to help my best friend's brother, I'd immersed myself in a world I know little about and invited god knows what into my life. I let out a deep breath and thought I should check in with Dr. Pereira. She was quickly becoming a trusted confidante, and I'd be wise to reach out to her when I felt myself start to unravel. I glanced at my phone to check the time, tossed my trash, and headed across campus for a workshop.

Cait was in Vegas, hard at work on her investigation of the casino owner and his extracurricular activities, and texted, asking if

I'd have time to talk that night. I told her that I'd be at home grading papers and looked forward to her call. After my usual evening activities of ball tossing in the backyard, dinner, and dishes, I settled on the couch with a cup of tea. Cait was prompt as always and wasted no time getting to the point after our hellos.

"I haven't talked to Daniel yet. He's still in Germany and apparently in a village that's too isolated to have reliable cell service, but I don't know if that means he can't call out at all or what. Anyway, I got a call from Evan, his business partner this morning."

"I didn't know he had a partner."

"Evan is more of a behind-the-scenes guy. While Daniel meets with buyers and sellers, Evan handles the accounting and insurance—the stuff that would drive Daniel crazy. I've only met him a few times, which is why it was so surprising to hear from him." She sounded worried.

"What did he want to talk to you about?"

"He hasn't heard from Daniel either. I guess they didn't talk before Daniel left for Germany. In fact, he said he didn't even know he was going.

"Okay, so that's odd but nothing to be too concerned about, right?

She paused. "Maybe not, but this is—Evan said he got a call from the bank this morning to verify that he had signed off on closing the corporate savings account. Evan didn't know anything about it."

"Whoa. How much was in the account?"

"About $75,000."

"Holy crap."

"Ash, I know this sounds really bad, but I know Daniel. There's no way he'd cheat Evan and run out on him."

"Let's not jump to conclusions," I said, wondering what could be going on that didn't point to shady behavior on Daniel's part. "Maybe there's a perfectly logical explanation."

"That's what I said, but Evan wasn't convinced. He said he's going to go to the police if he doesn't hear from Daniel by the end of the week. I can't let him do that."

"Well, hang on a minute, getting the police involved may call Daniel's character into question, but he's got nothing to worry about if he's done nothing wrong."

"I know, but I just don't think Evan should call the cops. He needs to give Daniel a chance to speak for himself."

"When will he be back?"

"I'm not sure. He didn't give me any details when we spoke before he left."

"I don't know what you can do until you're able to talk to him."

"Yeah, you're right…I just can't shake this feeling that Daniel needs my help."

"He's lucky to have you in his corner," I said, wondering how I'd handle things if I were in her shoes. She told me she'd be back in the valley the following week to check on her mother, who was recovering from a badly sprained ankle. We ended the conversation shortly after that, and I thought about how often finding answers only seems to raise more questions.

14

The tree-lined streets of East Sac are a thing to behold in the fall. English Elms, Live Oak, Japanese Maples, and Modesto Ash treat us to a stunning display of color. As Cody and I walked down the street on the way to the park for our morning run, I made a point to soak it all in and appreciate what I was seeing. It's far too easy to get caught up in the grind of daily life, not to mention major dramas like a murder investigation or Cait's mission to find out what was going on with Daniel, and completely miss the beauty of what's right in front of us. I looked at those magnificent trees and promised myself I'd make a concerted effort to avoid that.

We began to run, and I thought that might be a good way to open the Psych 101 lecture. I'd been trying to find more ways to connect what my students were reading in the text with what they were experiencing in their lives. It can be a challenge, especially in an introductory class, to connect the theoretical to the practical without losing much of the class. Reading Freud, Jung, and other luminaries for the first time, it's easy to get caught up in their various psychological theories and forget that they formed those theories after years of working with actual people. The ideologies spelled out in black and white seem disconnected from real life. I'm tasked with creating a bridge to join those two worlds and helping my students across.

Running down the path, I started to outline the lecture in my head, thinking about the main points I wanted to make. When I first started teaching, I doubted I'd ever be able to get through a lecture without detailed notes in front of me, regardless of what my favorite profs—the ones who made it look so easy—told me. And then, as is so often the case, the less I stressed about it, the easier it became. Talking about the responsibilities we all have seemed like a good place to start. Amid schoolwork, jobs, and housekeeping, a little mindfulness about the world around us does a world of good. Right on campus, we have the arboretum, the Guy West Bridge that spans the river, and squirrels that are so bold they'll steal your lunch if you aren't paying attention. Taking mini mental breaks, especially during your first year, can help keep you grounded.

It was a beautiful, cool, crisp morning. Cody trotted happily along beside me, showing no sign of tiring, making me wonder how long he'd keep running if I didn't have to get to work. I'd no doubt wear out first. As much as I enjoy autumn, the later sunrise forces me to forego running on my early days. Plenty of people do their morning runs in the dark, but that seems unwise for a woman, even with a dog. And after becoming involved with the investigation, it seemed extremely unwise for me. We rounded the corner onto my street, and I thought about my quiet little neighborhood, my friends going about their normal lives, and how somewhere in my city a murderer was no doubt planning his next gruesome attack. I'd best take my own advice about trying to stay grounded.

Later that morning, in the pop culture class, we discussed comics, graphic novels, and anime, led by two students who had self-published a graphic novel over the summer. They were quite proud of it, and rightly so, as it was very well done. We had a lively discussion, as are most in that class, but I was only half there. Could my students tell? I managed to make it through the class without embarrassing myself, and the rest of the day passed in a blur. I graded papers, met with students during my office hour, and chatted with Ang between classes. If she could tell I was distracted, she didn't mention it and let me be. My personality theory class passed without incident, and I'd made it through yet another distracted day.

Angelica, Tony, a department old-timer, and I walked out to the parking garage together through the early evening twilight. As an adjunct prof, Ang is somewhat removed from the fray as far as department politics. I tried not to whine too much to her, but she knew I'd been butting heads with the department chair. Tony surprised me by breaking his "no shop talk off the clock" rule when he said, "Hey, I know Lydia's on your back about attending more meetings and being *more engaged*." He made air quotes with an eye roll. How did he know that? I'd never once spoken to him about it.

"I know what's up, Ash. I've been around long enough to know how Lydia operates. You're not the first and you won't be the last one she's pushed."

I'd been watching my colleagues since Lydia told me I needed to learn to play the game. "How do you do it, Tony? I know you don't give a damn about the politics of the university. How do you make it look like you do?"

"It's a balancing act for the most part. I don't like the politics of this place any more than you do, which is why I chose a smaller school. I'd last about a day and a half at an Ivy League gig. So I show up for meetings, volunteer to lead a workshop or two, and Lydia is happy."

"But what about all the gossip and posturing?" I asked.

"You'll find that just about anywhere, and I can ignore it for the most part, though it's really kind of amusing when you think about it. You'd expect a group of psych profs to be a bit more self-aware."

Angelica laughed. "Good point."

We'd reached our cars by then.

"The main thing you have to remember, Ash, is that this is about performance. Most people are performing, and ninety-eight or so percent of us are driven by pride and ego."

"Thanks, Tony, this has been quite the pep talk," I said. "Seriously, though, I do appreciate your perspective."

He smiled. "All in a day's work. And I'll leave you with this—if you can find a way to make your boss happy without selling your soul or compromising your principles, you've got it made."

How true. We said our goodbyes, and I got into my car to head home.

*****

He ended the call and set down his phone. Wiping his palms on his jeans and trying to slow his pounding heart, he thought about what he needed to do. His only real option. It didn't matter how he got here; there was only one way out. Men like Romano didn't care about anything but protecting their own interests. His run of bad luck at the blackjack table had continued longer than any he'd ever experienced, and now, backed into a very dangerous corner, he had no choice but to accept Romano's offer to work off his debt by "helping out." He paced around the room, grabbed a bottle of water, and sipped, staring out the window. He really wanted a beer, but that was a bad idea. He needed to stay completely clearheaded, as he couldn't afford even the tiniest of mistakes.

It shouldn't take long to catch up; he wasn't really *that* far in the hole. So he'd move some funds around and cycle Romano's profits through his business. So what? No one would get hurt, and no one had to know, especially his partner. A victimless crime to be sure. He finished the water, opened his laptop, and got to work. Step one: placement. Start to move Romano's money into the operations account. Keeping the deposits under $10,000 is the rule everyone knows, but spreading them out to avoid anything that looks like a pattern would ensure that he stayed under the IRS radar. He'd make periodic deposits in random amounts and categorize them as consultation fees. That shouldn't be cause for concern. He often shared his professional opinion with people in the automotive world.

Step two, layering, was going to be a bit trickier, complicated by the fact that Romano dealt in cash much of the time. He'd need to use one of his offshore accounts where regulations and enforcement were a bit less rigorous. If he was slow and methodical, he could do it without attracting attention. Moving the money between various accounts would make it harder to follow should anyone become curious and investigate. The final step was funneling the cash back to Romano so he could introduce seemingly clean money into the system. Piece of cake. Take it slow, focus, don't get sloppy, and don't attract attention. If he could do that, he could get out from under his debt, and maybe Romano wouldn't break his knees—or worse.

*****

Cait called after dinner when I was settled on the couch with a stack of papers to grade.

"Hey, how's it going in Vegas?"

"Pretty well, actually. Of course, that's ignoring all the cigarette smoke, rude tourists, and the utter lack of anything real."

She'd neatly summed up everything I hate about that city. "Hard to believe people go there on purpose, isn't it?"

"It is, although I do intellectually understand the allure. Everything is so sensationalized you can pretend to be someone else and forget you have responsibilities."

"I guess I get that," I said. "It's just too over the top for me. Plus, it's in the desert."

"Depends on your definition of *desert*, my friend."

"Ah, good point." This from the woman who's been to Morocco and Afghanistan. "So what's going on with Casino Guy?"

"Apparently much more than originally suspected. It looks like he's running a car theft ring that's tied to some of the auto chop shops in West Sacramento."

"There are chop shops in West Sac?"

"Yeah, near the port where all those warehouses are."

That shouldn't surprise me. Enterprise and Industrial boulevards are lined with warehouses, and there are always plenty of trucks coming and going. The perfect place for an under-the-radar business.

"But why would this guy bother with Sacramento?" I asked. "Surely there are plenty of cars to steal in Nevada."

"Because of the port."

The port of West Sacramento ships literal tons of rice, barley, wheat, corn, and almonds all over the world. It also handles cement, clay, and heavy machinery.

"What does our port have to do with cars? It mostly ships agricultural crops—it was initially built to service the Northern California rice industry."

"True, and that's still your major export, but here's where it gets interesting," she said. "The West Sac port can handle large cargo ships because of the deep-water channel, but it doesn't have the giant cranes like the ones you see in Oakland, so it can't handle those huge shipping containers. Some cars do come into Sac via the port. They call that shipping method 'roll on, roll off,' which is just what it sounds like and obviously makes the cars easier to steal."

Interesting indeed. "Okay, so they're easier to steal than if they were in containers, but they still have to get them off the ship."

"True, but if the guy in charge of the receiving logs can be paid to look the other way, or better yet, if he works at the shop, too, the cars come into West Sacramento but never make it to the dealers. Within hours, the parts are on their way back out."

"Damn. This guy must be making bank," I said, thinking of the Mercedes and Jaguar dealerships in town.

"Definitely. The feds think he's guilty of money laundering, too, and he's under intense scrutiny, but they haven't been able to prove it yet."

"Wow, this is getting really intense. You sure it's still safe?"

"Thanks for the concern, but I got this."

"Okay," I said, not sure I meant it. "How much longer are you going to be there?"

"I'm leaving tomorrow night."

I was really worried about how complicated Cait's investigation was becoming, but I told myself it mostly had to do with my disdain for Vegas. Besides, I knew how she'd react to my casting stones, since I was in an equally complicated, if not dangerous, situation myself.

"Have you been able to talk to Daniel?"

"No, not yet. We played phone tag today. I finally googled Haueneberstein, the village he's staying in. It's on the northwest edge of the Black Forest, and they've had some severe storms over the past week. The main road that leads out is completely blocked by a mudslide."

"Oh damn. So he's stuck there and has lousy cell service, and you haven't been able to get a hold of him."

"Yep," she said, her voice heavy with worry.

"I'm sure he's fine."

"Yeah, me too I just..."

"You need to talk to him and hear his voice."

"Exactly."

We spent a few more minutes on the phone and then said good night.

15

As Angelica and I walked out to the parking garage together, it struck me just how few lights there were on campus. Had it always been this dark at night? I decided I was just jumpy since I was now thinking about the investigation all the time. She didn't seem to notice, chatting away about her last class. Ang and I were on our way to a new club in Midtown to see my friend Stephen's band, Evolution Theory, play. For the record, if I were ten years younger, I'd consider breaking my "no dating musicians" rule for Stephen. He's sweet, funny, and extremely talented. He's also very handsome and quite the flirt. Angelica and I don't have a lot in common when it comes to music, but she's always open to hearing something new, and she'd had a rough few weeks, thanks to a problem student, so she was up for a fun night out.

When we arrived at Backstage Pass, the band was still setting up. We were deciding where to sit when I heard a familiar voice.

"Ashley?"

I turned to see another old friend from my Tower days.

"Ian! What brings you to town?"

"You're looking at it," he said, gesturing at the room with a sweep of his arm.

"Seriously? This is yours? Congratulations!"

I introduced Angelica, and Ian went on to tell us that he decided to come back to Sacramento when the opportunity to buy the club came up. There had been talk of cutbacks at the record label he'd worked for in Los Angeles for the past few years, so he took a buyout package, made the move, and he and a colleague who'd also seen the writing on the wall went in together and opened what they hoped would provide a boost to the Sacramento music scene. Leading us to a table near the stage and removing a "Reserved" sign, he said, "You get a VIP table, of course."

"Why thank you, sir," Ang said.

"My pleasure." He took a sip from the oversized mug he was holding.

"Tea is still your one and only vice? I guess some things never change," I said. Back in our record store days, Ian was rarely seen without a travel mug of tea, whether he was stocking his sections or running a cash register. The coffee drinkers teased him, and one of the day managers bought him a dainty china cup and saucer, but he took even more crap about being a teetotaler. In the permissive, anything goes atmosphere of Tower, not to mention the record industry in general, alcohol was woven into the fabric of the culture.

"Why change now?" he asked.

"A club owner who doesn't drink. You just have to be different, don't you?"

He grinned. "Can't help being awesomely original. It's great to see you, Ash, but I really should go play host. I'll be back in a bit."

"Work the room, dude," I said, hugging him. "Thanks for the preferred seating. It's great to see you, Ian, and congrats again. I'm really happy for you."

"Thanks," he said. "I'm really excited to see what we can do with this place. He turned and headed toward the entrance.

Stephen and the band had finished setting up by then, and he came over to say hello, greeting us with a big smile.

"Hey, Ash, so glad you could make it!" he said, hugging me.

I introduced him to Ang and then said, "It takes a lot to make me miss one of your shows."

"I know, that's what makes you a super fan."

We sat down and spent a few minutes catching up, and then he asked how I knew Ian.

"We worked at the record store together. He went to LA to work for a label after I transferred to the marketing department, and we were his main account. I'd heard he was considering a move to

New York for a while, but we lost touch after I left Tower, so I didn't know he was back in town."

"Just out of curiosity," Stephen said, "how many people do you know who didn't work for Tower at some point?"

"That's a good question," Angelica said. "I've been wondering about that myself."

"Counting you two? Let's see…" I rolled my eyes to the ceiling and began to tally imaginary people on my fingers.

"You're hilarious," Ang said.

I shrugged. "Ten years, 2,700 or so people…you do the math."

Stephen glanced toward the stage and said it was about time for them to get started. "Nice meeting you," he said, reaching across the table to shake Angelica's hand. He leaned over, kissed my cheek, and said he'd be back between sets.

"He's a sweetheart," she said as he walked away.

"He certainly is," I agreed, thinking he was that and much more.

Ang offered to go to the bar, saying we could get away with an occasional indulgence on a weeknight. I agreed and settled back to people-watch before the show began. Introvert that I am, the club scene was never my thing, even in college, but I am fascinated by watching extroverts become animated and draw energy from the very thing that exhausts me.

Ian came by to introduce his partner before the show started. They're physical opposites, with Jeff looking to be at least six foot two, in contrast to Ian's five-six frame. (Years ago, during a particularly slow-closing shift, Ian and I measured ourselves and discovered we're precisely the same height). Jeff's rich ebony skin tone made Ian's fair complexion and ice-blue eyes look even paler. But their personalities appear to be a perfect match. Jeff is every bit as animated as Ian and equally at home playing host, greeting people, and keeping an eye on the door.

"Great meeting you both," he said. "Enjoy the show."

We assured him we would and then turned our attention to the stage as the music began.

Ang ended up enjoying the music so much she bought a CD and wanted to hang out with the band after the show, which I'm always up for. If there was one thing I could change about myself, it would be to have any kind of musical talent. I'm so envious of people who can just pick up an instrument and play or sit down and write a song. We were chatting over wine and various cocktails when Jesse texted. I would normally ignore my phone when out with friends, but life had been anything but normal since I started working with Ed and Jesse. I surreptitiously checked it and got a raised eyebrow from Angelica. She doesn't miss much. I quickly replied, telling Jesse where I was, that I'd make an excuse, and be at the station within twenty minutes. I made my apologies to the table, got a goodbye hug from Stephen, and on the way out told Ang I'd explain in the car.

I had intended to keep my involvement in the investigation from everyone at the university, including my office mate, but as I'd discovered the day I found a rat in my mail, that was becoming increasingly difficult. I had just pulled away from the curb when she said, "Okay, spill it."

I sighed, trying to think of the most succinct way to explain what was going on without saying anything I wasn't authorized to talk about.

"I've told you about my college roommate."

"The journalist? Yeah, you talk about her a lot."

"Well, her brother is the one who came to the office the day I found that rat in the mail. He's a police detective, who is currently in the middle of a rather high-profile investigation."

I went on to explain that I was acting as a consultant and, given that it was an open investigation, I couldn't talk about any pertinent details.

She was silent for a moment and then said, "Wait, you're serious—this isn't a joke."

"No, it's not."

"A high-profile case—holy crap! Not the murder investigation? The one that's at the top of the local news every night?"

"I can neither confirm nor deny that," I said, cringing at how completely ridiculous I sounded.

"Ashley, this is huge, not to mention totally freaky. Is it even safe for you to be doing this? Ohmigod! Do you think it was the killer who sent you that rat?"

"We don't know. I still think it was probably a prank," I said, even though I no longer believed that. "But Jesse wouldn't let me be in any danger. The media has no idea I'm involved, so there's no way the killer—or killers," I added quickly, "would have any way of finding out."

"Man, I hope you're right."

You and me both, I thought. We were quiet for the rest of the fifteen-minute drive to her house.

As I pulled into her driveway, Ang thanked me for introducing her to such a great band. We said our goodbyes, and I headed for the station.

Ed's mood was dark when Jesse and I sat down at the conference room table.

"Sorry to pull you away from your friends," Jesse said.

"Please don't worry about it. When I said I was in, I didn't mean just when it was convenient. Am I right in assuming our guy struck again?"

"Unfortunately, yes," Ed answered. About three hours ago, a thirty-nine-year-old woman was found behind the Catholic church downtown. Cause of death was strangulation."

Jesse started to remove the photos from the murder book when I stopped him.

"Wait. Did he…was she…sexually assaulted?"

"No. And I would have told you if that had been the case before I showed you the photos."

I realized I'd been holding my breath. I didn't think that was in our creep's wheelhouse, but then this was his first female victim.

When Jesse asked if I was ready to go on, I nodded. But before he revealed the photos, he said, "Did you have a chance to meet with Dr. Pereira yet?"

I told him I had and that we'd had a good discussion.

"And you'll call her if you need to talk about…whatever?"

"Yes. She insisted that we keep in touch."

"Good deal. Okay, ready to get on with this so we don't keep you here all night?"

"Yeah, let's take a look."

He placed two black-and-white photos of the victim in front of me. The woman was sitting with her back against the wall of the church, slumped forward with her head resting on her bent knees, as if she were asleep. Her purse was by her feet, and there was play money from a children's board game scattered all around. I ran my hand through my hair, wondering what on earth that could mean. There were plenty of songs about money, greed, and corruption, but this woman was behind a church. Then I noticed something else next to her purse.

"Guys…is that a fish?"

"Yeah. As in fish on Friday, right?" Jesse said.

"Maybe…fish and fake money. Good lord, I have no idea what to make of this one."

Perhaps our psycho was already tired of his game and had invented a completely new one. Or maybe he was done with music and had moved on to movies, television, or god knows what. Whatever he was doing, more people were falling victim to his twisted psyche, and Jesse had placed his faith in me to help figure out how to find the creep. And I had absolutely no idea how to do that. Not a clue. We spent the next half hour going through the initial report and pondering the photos and sketches of the crime scene. By then, it was nearly eleven thirty.

Jesse yawned and stretched. "Let's call it a night."

"Excellent idea, partner," Eduardo said.

I nodded. "I agree."

Jesse put the information back into the murder book and asked me if I was okay to drive home.

"What? Yeah, I'm fine. I had a couple glasses of wine at the club, but that was hours ago."

"That's not what I mean. It's late and you're going to drive home alone after discussing murder and looking at crime scene photos."

Oh, that. "I'm okay, really. But thanks."

"Why don't I follow you home just to be safe. I'd feel better."

"You sure? I don't want to take you out of your way," I said but had no idea where Jesse lived.

"You're in East Sac, I'm in River Park. We're practically neighbors."

The three of us walked out to the parking lot together, and I was more relieved than I was willing to admit about Jesse's vigilance. That clinical sense of detachment I pride myself on was getting harder to hold on to.

16

He had been up all night, wandering around the city, following the Other's lead. Once the subject was chosen, he had to find a location that was precisely right for the event. Then he had to think about the story he was going to tell and choose exactly the right props. There was much work to be done, but the plan was coming together. He walked into a café and got in line with the normals to buy a cup of coffee. It was so easy to pretend he was like them. Little did they know of the power he commanded, the things he was capable of. Losers. He took his coffee outside, walked down the block, and sat on a low wall in front of the police station. Speaking of losers, here he was, in broad daylight, right in front of their fat cop noses! He giggled and a woman walking by turned to look at him. He should teach her to mind her own damned business, but he had bigger things to think about, like how he was going to deal with that pesky outside expert the cops had brought in.

It had been ridiculously easy to figure out who it was. Once the idiots on cable news started speculating about the university, he'd hung around on campus, scouted the faculty parking garage, and then, almost by accident, saw the same dark blue vintage Mustang he'd admired on campus parked at the police station. After that, it was just a matter of finding an unobtrusive vantage point from which to observe the faculty garage, get a visual on the driver, check the university website, and bingo—"expert" identified. He'd fired an opening volley to see if he could scare her off. If that didn't do it, he'd have to turn up the heat. College types…they always think they're so smart, so much better than everyone else. They'd learn—all of them. They'd all see what he and the Other could do.

Later that day, he walked across campus as if he belonged there, disappearing into the crowds of students hurrying between buildings. If he didn't make eye contact, no one noticed him. He felt as though he were invisible. He liked that; it made him feel like a superhero, which he truly was, thanks to the Other. He relished the idea of walking around campus, completely anonymous, on the turf of the busybody helping the cops. He walked past a nondescript building and heard a student call it the psych building. Ah, the psychologists, they all thought they could figure out what was going on in his mind, blaming his childhood and saying ridiculous things about his mother. Such utter nonsense.

He'd been playing psychologists most of his life, starting with that moron at his elementary school who wanted him to tell her why he was angry and wanted to hit the other children. She didn't much care for his "because they're stupid" answer. He quickly learned how to figure out what grown-ups wanted to hear. They were easy to manipulate, especially if he acted scared instead of angry. They would go on about how he was safe and didn't need to be afraid, but he needed to tell them about the bad thoughts. If he told them, the bad thoughts couldn't hurt him. But they didn't understand; he could never tell them about the Other. Even when it was quiet for years at a time, he knew he was never alone.

He saw a security guard approaching, dropped his eyes, and acted as though he were just another professor on his way to class. Don't make eye contact and you're invisible. It's as easy as that. Another thing he'd learned as a child. The guard walked by without a glance. Some security—what a joke! He felt the energy coursing through his body and knew he was invincible. He could get rid of the annoying expert without much effort—she was a minor distraction at most—and get back to the task at hand: completing his mission and pleasing the Other. The power was deliciously intoxicating.

*****

Cody and I were out on our morning run when a thought stopped me in the middle of the path. I took my phone out of my pocket and looked up my suspicion. Bull's-eye. I called Jesse but got his voice mail. *Dammit!* I left a message asking him to call me as soon as possible. I went on with the run, my mind racing. Our sicko was obviously stepping up his game. My phone rang as we were walking up my driveway.

"Jesse, the woman behind the church, does the report say what kind of fish was found at the scene?"

"What kind of fish? I don't think so. Why?"

"I think it's a herring, an actual red herring," I said, letting us into the house.

"Oh, for God's sake, this guy is too much. I'll check it out when I get to the station, but I bet you're right. Hey, where does that term come from, anyway?"

"It's long been used in literature and fiction, especially mysteries, to mean anything that diverts attention from the central issue, but it alludes to dragging a smoked—which is apparently what turns them red—herring across a trail to throw the bloodhounds off."

"No kidding? Wow, the things I'm learning hanging out with you," he said. "So if the red herring is meant to divert us and has nothing to do with the woman behind the church, can we assume the board game money doesn't either?"

"Yeah, I bet we can."

"Then what *does* it mean?"

"I don't know. The money could represent just about anything to do with greed or material possessions, and I'm sure the killer is raising the stakes, looking for that bigger rush. Maybe he's making his riddles more complicated to—oh god," I said as a bone-chilling thought occurred.

"What?"

"Jesse, what if it's a hint as to what he's going to do next?"

His voice came out strained. "Good god. We have got to outsmart this bastard and find him! I need to get going and get into the station, but thanks, Ashley. We're making progress. I know it doesn't feel like it, but I swear to you we are."

He was right. It didn't feel like we were getting anywhere. We said our goodbyes and planned to talk later in the day. I went about my morning routine, showering and getting ready for work, but it was becoming increasingly difficult to keep my head in the game. I'd have to work to stay focused on my classes. I made a mental note to check in with Colleen, hoping she'd at least have time for a phone call.

As it happened, the good doctor reached out to me between classes before I had a chance to call her, wanting to know if I was up for trivia that evening. I told her I absolutely was and asked if she had a moment to talk. Fortunately, she was between patients and had a few minutes to spare. She asked what was going on. I hesitated, reaching for the words to explain what I was feeling.

"Well, it's just that...I'm having an increasingly difficult time staying focused at work. The investigation is on my mind all the time, and I feel like not only am I not very invested in my job but that I'm short-changing my students, and I really don't like that."

"That's to be expected to a certain extent, Ashley. You're dealing with a very traumatic situation, and you're confronting some cruel realities about what human beings are capable of for the first time. My honest opinion is that you're actually doing very well, no doubt due to your background."

I had to smile. "If this is doing well, I don't think I want to know what struggling would look like."

"I get that," she said. "But seriously, you can't expect not to be affected by something of this magnitude. I know you had no way of knowing what you were in for and how involved the investigation would become, but did you really think you'd be able to leave it at the station after meeting with Jesse and Ed?"

I paused. "I didn't think about that at all, but I suppose if you'd asked me when I first agreed to get involved, I would have said that I could."

"You know what? I'm sure I would've, too, in the same situation."

That surprised me. "Really?"

"Really. I think you know, Ashley, that even those of us in this profession aren't immune to thinking we can handle whatever life throws at us. But I'd like you to remember that the way to deal with this is to talk about it. Granted, the circle of people you can chat with about the investigation is quite small—just Jesse, Ed, and me—but please reach out to us. Call me, text Jesse, do what you need to when you feel like it's taking over and keeping you from focusing."

I thanked her for her time and compassion and said I'd see her that evening at the café for trivia. I lowered my phone and let out a breath, thinking I was extremely fortunate to have someone with Dr. Pereira's insight and background in my corner.

Later that evening, at the midtown café that hosts a biweekly trivia night, I learned that Colleen and her friends—Stephanie, a literary agent, Gail, a curator at the Crocker Museum, and Jen, a high school history teacher—are a very competitive bunch. They were there to have fun and blow off some steam, but they were also planning to win. Colleen had chosen her team carefully, covering literature, art, and world history. Recruiting me to handle music and pop culture was a very calculated move. As we chatted before the first game began, I found myself really enjoying hearing about worlds so different from my own, like publishing and the museum. Stephanie told us about a submission she'd received from a young man pitching his "three-part trilogy."

"Unfortunately for him," she said, "his pitch letter was the highlight of his work."

When the host called for quiet and said it was time to begin, all friendly banter at the table ended. My teammates were ready to go, and I sincerely hoped I wouldn't let them down. As luck would have it, questions in the first round included the title of an early Beatles B-side ("I'll Get You," which backed "She Loves You"), a scene from *Blade Runner*, (Deckard's pursuit of Zhora through crowded futuristic LA streets, culminating with her death), and a *South Park* quote (Cartman's "I know enough to exploit it" when the guys question his choice to start a Christian rock band), allowing me to show off and earn instant cred with my new acquaintances. Fun stuff. It was a great evening, and I was able to relax and enjoy the company of some fabulous women, be in the moment, and, most importantly, stop thinking about the investigation for a few hours.

The next day, I was in my office talking to a grad student about her research project when the department admin dropped off the mail. I rarely had anything of note delivered at the university, and I'd been a little jumpy since receiving the rat, wondering if the sender was going to follow up with another creepy surprise. I tried to pay attention to my student; she was one of my favorites, but my eyes kept wandering to the stack of magazines and envelopes on the corner of my desk. *Focus.*

"Professor McKennitt, are you okay?"

"I'm sorry, Christy, I'm fine... I just got a lousy night's sleep. Please continue."

She smiled and I wished I could reassure myself as easily. "Okay, so as you know, I'm studying name recall and how effective the classic mnemonic devices are. You know, the ones like, if you meet a Mrs. Crocker, you're supposed to picture her with a giant cookbook."

"Yes, those have been tossed around for decades. Have you ever used one?"

"No," she said. "I've tried but I can never think of anything clever on the spot, and I end up not only immediately forgetting the person's name but also missing half of what they've just told me. How do you remember our names?"

"To be honest, sometimes I don't. It seems like every semester, there's one student I just can't get a name to stick to. But I do have the benefit of the class roster, and I often make a note by the names to help me remember. And of course, the more you guys talk in class and I get to know your personalities, the easier it becomes."

She nodded. "That makes sense."

"Besides, I've discovered that students tend to sit in the same desks throughout a semester. Were you annoyed in high school if a teacher created a seating chart?"

"Yes! I hated that."

"But when you were allowed to sit anywhere you wanted, did you move around the room?"

"No. I think I sat at the same desk every day."

"I'm sure I did too. It's human nature to seek the comfort of routine, even something as simple as where you choose to sit in a classroom."

"Isn't that fascinating? Guess that's why I'm a psych major."

"Yep, and as I've said before, welcome to the club."

We finished going over the particulars of her project and how best to present her findings, and then she was off to the library.

I took a deep breath and reached for the mail, not seeing anything out of the ordinary. So far so good. A few trade journals, the department newsletter, and a little five-by-seven padded envelope. There was no return address, stamp, or postage, just "Prof McKennitt" printed in block letters. It certainly wasn't big enough to contain a rat, but there could have been something equally gross inside, like spiders, which would make me completely lose it. After studying the envelope for a moment, I realized it felt like it was just a CD. I'd had enough sent to me in my Tower days I was sure that was what I'd find inside. I sliced open the envelope and found *Faith* by The Cure. No note or anything else, just the CD. Weird. A student might have dropped it off to listen to and discuss in the pop culture class, but it was odd there wasn't a note. I put it back into the envelope and dropped it in my desk drawer, thinking I may want to mention it to Jesse later.

I walked into my office after lunch and realized I'd left my phone on my desk. That was something I didn't often do. Increasingly distracted as the case progressed, I found myself thinking about it nearly all the time, mostly in abstract terms, as I considered the killer's motivations, wondering what was driving him and what new puzzles he might be concocting for us. But more often lately, and quite suddenly, I'd be hit with the realization that a serial killer was loose in my city and was wandering around right at that moment, possibly looking for his next victim. I then got a chill I couldn't shake. Jesse had texted while I was out. He wanted me to meet him at the station after work. He didn't need to tell me what that meant.

Angelica walked in as I was tapping out a reply. She saw my expression and said, "You texting your cop?"

I nodded.

"But you can't tell me what you're discussing."

"That's right."

"I get that," she said, "but when this whole thing is over, I'd better be the first one you clue in, and I mean everything."

"Deal," I said, wondering how much she'd really want to know and how much I'd feel I could share. I hadn't yet decided if my department colleagues would be more able to handle the grisly details due to their backgrounds or less so because of their foundation of understanding aberrant behaviors. The practical meeting the theoretical is not always welcome.

We chatted for a few minutes about university happenings and the usual campus politics, and then it was time for her office hours and for me to get to class.

I walked into the station that evening, and the desk clerk just handed me my visitor's pass and buzzed Jesse, hardly glancing up. When the detective came to get me, I could see the toll the investigation was taking on him. He looked somber, exhausted, and ten years older. We sat down at the table in the conference room, and he opened the binder in front of him.

"You were right on the mark with the idea that the board game money was a hint about what our creep was going to do next."

Ed joined us as Jesse took three photos out of the binder, placed them on the table, and continued. "A sixty-five-year-old bank executive was found in his office this morning by a teller. Time of death was sometime between ten o'clock last night and two o'clock this morning. Cause of death has initially been ruled suffocation, pending the autopsy and toxicology report."

The man was sitting at his desk, lifeless eyes staring straight ahead. Jesse continued reading the report, which stated that the man was likely suffocated with a plastic bag.

"Is that why his skin tone looks so odd?" I asked.

"No. I know I shouldn't speak ill of the dead, but this guy had the worst spray tan I've ever seen. His skin was orange."

"You'd think a bank manager could afford better."

"That's what I thought," Eduardo said, "but given the really bad toupee, he must have been a real cheapskate."

"Money doesn't necessarily equal style or good taste," I said.

"Obviously." Jesse agreed.

We spent the next several minutes going over the report and looking at the sketch of the crime scene and the rest of the photos. There were a few river rocks on the man's desk, and there was a life jacket on the floor, the straps of which had been cut. My mind was abuzz with thoughts of drowning, sinking, fighting for life. What was this sick little scene supposed to be telling us?

"What do you think?" Jesse asked.

"Well, the river rock and life jacket suggest drowning, but that seems too easy. Then again, with two rivers and Folsom Lake, there are an awful lot of places our guy could stage one of his dramas. It seems like…"

"What?"

"Maybe…maybe he could be connecting two scenes—this one and whatever he's planning to do next. This guy," I said, pointing at the photo, "was suffocated, as far as we know, which is not that different from drowning. What if that's sort of a lead-in to his next act, which is a drowning? There's a song by The Cure—oh my god…"

"What's wrong?" Ed asked.

I tried and failed to keep my voice steady. "When the department admin brought my mail today, there was one of those padded envelopes with a CD by The Cure in it. It didn't have a postmark or a label, just 'Prof McKennitt' handwritten in block letters. I assumed that a student dropped it off for the pop culture class."

"Do you still have it?" Jesse asked.

"Yeah, it's in my desk drawer. I really did intend to mention it to you, and then the day got away from me. Anyway, one of the songs is called 'The Drowning Man,' but in the song, it's a woman who drowns, and the man just feels like he's drowning."

Ed looked as though he were having trouble maintaining his composure. "So the killer was on campus and probably in your building? Can people who have no business there just wander around freely? Is your office locked when you're in class? How would someone get something to you without sending it through the mail?"

I took a breath and tried to answer each of his questions. "No one checks for campus IDs, so anyone can walk into most of the buildings. The office is locked when neither Angelica nor I are there. There's an intracampus mail system, but the CD was just in a plain envelope with my name on it. I suppose he could have just left it in the building somewhere and someone would have taken it to the admin."

"But he was almost definitely in your building."

"Yeah," I said, feeling an icy tingle in my stomach.

Jesse put his head in his hands. "So the killer has been in your building, and it's likely that a woman is going to drown, and we're going to be a step behind and unable to save her."

I couldn't bring myself to answer and just nodded.

Ed had been watching Jesse closely. "Jess...maybe you need to take five."

Ignoring his partner, Jesse said, "Let me ask you something, Ashley. If I were referred to you, if you were going to be my therapist and I came to you with this bag of headaches, what would you tell me? How would you advise me to cope?"

I paused for a moment before saying, "I'd start by telling you what you already know. That there are monsters in this world, that evil does exist, and there are times when the good guys don't win." I couldn't help but think of the scene in *Alien* where the little girl tells Sigourney Weaver that there really are monsters. "But for every one of those times, there are at least ten when good does prevail over evil and the good guys triumph. I'd encourage you to share every dark, creepy, scary thought that comes into your mind because by exposing those thoughts to the light, you diminish their power. You signed up to be one of the good guys, and you're not alone. We're in this together, and we're going to see it through to the end together."

"You're good," he said. "In fact, you sound like Dr. Pereira. Thank you for that. One more question, and I know I've asked before, but I need you to tell me again. Are you sorry I dragged you into this? Be honest with me."

I hesitated. "Yes and no. No, because I'm still fascinated with this investigation from a clinical perspective, and I am thinking of writing one hell of a research paper, thanks to all this hands-on expe-rience. And yes, because…it's taken over my every thought and is affecting the way I look at the world. I'm seeing potential monsters everywhere I look."

"Like I said from the beginning, say the word and you're out. No explanation or apology necessary."

Would it be smart to walk? Probably. I took another deep breath, let it out, and shook my head. "No. I'm in. We see this through together."

He smiled, and for the first time in weeks, I saw not an exhausted detective but a hint of the thirteen-year-old I once knew.

"And with that, I suggest we call it a night," Ed said.

He got no argument from either of us. We walked out into the chilly night air, and without even mentioning it, Jesse followed me home. He waited until he saw me go into the house and then tapped his horn, waved, and drove away.

17

I was in my office answering emails when Angelica came in after her clinical psych class. We chatted about the day-to-day happenings around campus for a bit, and then she said, "I think I have a pretty good shot at a permanent position here next year."

"Really? That's great! When did they tell you?"

"I met with the department chair and the board this morning. Apparently, they've been discussing it but didn't want me to get my hopes up in case it didn't pan out."

"That's fantastic, congrats. Anything I can do to help make sure it happens?" Since I was lucky enough to be hired on as permanent faculty when I started at Sac State, I wasn't sure about the route from adjunct to full-time professor.

"Would you be willing to write a letter of recommendation?"

"Consider it done. Anything else?"

"That's it for the moment, but I'll let you know if I think of something."

"You'd better. I'm really happy for you, Ang. This is great news and it's well deserved."

She gave me one of her room-brightening smiles. "Thanks. What's the latest with the investigation you're not supposed to talk about?"

"Nothing I can tell you, smart-ass."

She laughed. "I had to try. You might let something slip one of these days."

I smiled but I had to wonder how much Angelica and Cait, the only other person who knew of my involvement with the investigation, would really want to know if they had the opportunity to see the things I'd seen and confront the depths of cruelty our fellow humans can be capable of.

"As I've promised you, when it's all over, you'll be among the first to get the whole scoop."

"Well, I guess I'll have to live with that, "she said. "Speaking of the thing you're not supposed to speak of, have you gotten any more nasty gifts in the mail?"

"No, not since the rat."

I hadn't told Ang about the Cure CD. Yet another reason I was looking forward to the investigation being over was so I didn't have to keep track of what I had and hadn't told my office mate. I think Mark Twain is credited with saying if you tell the truth, you don't have to remember anything. Well said, Mr. Clemens, well said.

"Thank goodness for that. Did you ever find out where the rat came from? I mean, you know, if it was from the…guy?" She glanced at the doorway.

"No, there's really no way to tell. Jesse assumes he sent it, and I think so, too, but we can't prove that, so…"

"Wow." She was quiet a moment and then said, "Hey, you're still safe, right? And your cop can protect you?"

"Absolutely," I said, wishing I believed it.

I thanked Ang for her concern, gathered my notes, and headed across campus to my personality theory class.

The end of daylight-saving time always messes with me. I hate leaving work when it's already dark out. And since we keep pushing the start and end dates further apart, why don't we just get rid of it altogether? The one benefit I can name is that for at least a few weeks, my students have little trouble making it to an eight-o'clock class on time. I drove over to the police station through post-workday traffic and joined Jesse and Ed, who were sitting in the conference room brainstorming. All the murder books were on the table, and we were going over the particulars of each crime. The detectives were looking for anything that might tie the victims together, which would help them flesh out their profile of the killer. Completely random victims that have absolutely nothing to do with each other are a homicide detective's worst nightmare.

Jesse picked up the cold case report detailing the man found in the car by the old arena.

"This guy's occupation is listed as 'music distribution.' What does that mean, like a warehouse gig?"

"No," I said. "There are three major distribution companies that handle the big record labels—Universal, Sony, and Warner. There used to be more, but the changes in the industry brought about by the shift toward digital resulted in consolidation and mergers. Anyway, the label is what you'd see on a CD, like Columbia, which is owned and distributed by Sony. This guy was most likely a salesman, who called on accounts, wrote orders, and possibly handled advertising too."

"Like someone you would've worked with at Tower," Ed said.

"Yes, exactly."

He put on a pair of readers and skimmed the report on the man who was found in Discovery Park by the runners.

"This guy looks like a jack-of-all-trades. He sold insurance, did bookkeeping on the side, and was part owner of a club downtown."

I hadn't yet voiced my suspicion, but it was confirmed when Jesse said that the man found at the motel was the manager of a band from Los Angeles. The victims were connected, at least tangentially, by music. I was about to speak up when Jesse went on to say that the woman found behind the church worked for a company that owns many of the radio stations in town.

"They all have something to do with the music business," I said.

Jesse nodded, but Eduardo said, "Not so fast. This guy"—he held up a report—"was a bank manager."

"Okay," I began, "but he could've turned our guy down for a loan or repossessed his gear…"

"Or any number of things that link back to his being involved in music," Jesse finished.

"I guess that's possible." Detective Marquez wasn't completely convinced, but it was nice to have Jesse in my corner.

"If the music biz isn't the link," I said, "what else do the victims have in common?"

"Maybe finance ties them all together," Ed began and then held up a hand. "Hang on, Jess, let me finish. If our guy is a loan broker, or even a financial advisor, he may have had dealings with all of the victims."

Jesse was shaking his head. "No offense, partner, but I don't think that's the connection."

Ed shrugged. "Hey, I'm just tossing stuff at the wall to see what sticks." Then he looked at me and said, "What?"

"Um…well, if you're on board with the riddles the killer is leaving relating to music…"

"I am. I already said I'm with you on that." He sounded impatient.

"Then I don't see him being in finance. That just doesn't fit."

"I have to agree, Detective," Jesse said.

Ed sighed. "I sense I'm being double-teamed. But okay, I suppose you're right that it would make more sense for our guy to be in some sort of music-related occupation."

Sitting there in the conference room of the police station, I had one of those odd moments when the theoretical morphs into the concrete. While I'd been quite aware that the killer was roaming around doing mortal harm to innocent victims since we'd been profiling him, I'd been thinking about him in abstract terms. Discussing the possibility of him being someone involved in music, the industry I'd grown up working in, suddenly made him seem even more real and way too close for comfort.

*****

My neighbor, Linda, invited me to go to a new yoga class with her the following day. I've practiced yoga intermittently for years but, since adopting Cody, have been reluctant to commit to a regular class since I already feel bad about leaving him alone all day. But I enjoy Linda's company and knew the distraction would be good for me. I met her after work at a little place on H Street that had recently been remodeled and converted to a studio. Linda, who is a fabulous artist, met the instructor, Tané, through a gallery owner they've both dealt with. The East Sac artist community is a tight group—yet another thing I like about where I live. We were early, so after introductions, Linda and I chatted with Tané for a few minutes about Thanksgiving and the usual—what I did for a living, where I lived, and if I had done yoga before.

By then, more people had shown up, and two women walked in, discussing the investigation, which was still mentioned on the news nearly every night. So much for being distracted, I thought. I can't even get away from the case in the sanctity of a yoga studio.

"I still can't believe what's going on," Linda said. "There's a killer running around the city—our city—and they can't catch him."

"It's horrifying for sure," Tané agreed. "I don't want to be rude, but I kind of want to tell those women not to talk about it in here. We really don't want that kind of energy in the building. Do you think that's too pushy?"

Linda and I shook our heads. "No. It's your class. You get to make the rules," she said.

"I agree," I said. "Besides, aren't we supposed to leave the concerns of the day at the door?" Neither of them had any idea how badly I wanted to do that.

"We are, indeed. Thank you," Tané said. "Okay, I think everyone who's coming tonight is here, so I'll get started. Nice meeting you, Ashley." I said the same and thanked her for accommodating my last-minute attendance.

Linda and I had claimed space on the floor before most of the class showed up. We unrolled our mats as Tané welcomed everyone with a kind smile. She handled the no-negativity issue by tactfully suggesting that the yoga studio is the place to cultivate peace of mind, body, and spirit, which can best be accomplished by leaving the pressing matters of daily life outside and turning our attention inward.

"Your cares and worries will be there if you want to pick them back up on your way out," she said. "But hopefully they'll be lighter, or better yet, you may decide you don't need to pick them up again at all." She was good.

After a brief warmup, we spent forty-five minutes working through various sun salutation sequences and focusing on breathing with the poses flowing into one another, one per breath. It was fabulous. I was able to get out of my head and forget about the investigation, my research paper, and campus politics, at least temporarily. I would do well to come back. Tané turned out to be a very hands-on instructor, circulating through the class and offering gentle corrections on poses when needed. We ended class with a guided meditation and the total relaxation of Savasana. I thanked Tané for a great class and received a warm hug. I realized that she'd created a world for herself, full of positivity, light, and love. That was something to be admired and not unattainable if I chose to put in the effort. Linda and I walked out into the cold night together, and I thanked her for suggesting I join her.

"Sure thing, I'm glad you enjoyed the class."

"I really did and I'm going to make an effort to fit it into my schedule."

I didn't tell her how very much I needed to make that happen.

The next afternoon, I was in my office grading papers when the department admin dropped off the mail. I still had quite a few to read, so I should've ignored the distraction, but the things I'd been sent had me looking for more at every turn. I quickly sorted the stack and didn't see anything out of the ordinary. Big sigh of relief. I turned back to the student's paper, and Angelica walked in with an intracampus envelope.

"This is for you. It was mistakenly delivered to Tony's office."

I didn't reach out to take the mailer, forcing Ang to drop it on my desk. University policy dictates that intracampus mail must be sent in so-designated manila envelopes, which it was. My name was neatly printed in the "To" column next to a blank space under "From," and I was spooked enough not to want to open it. I debated briefly and then shoved it aside with my pen, pretending that I'd be able to concentrate on grading papers with it sitting there. I lasted an entire seventeen minutes, for which I congratulated myself. Picking up the mailer by a corner, I flipped it over, unfastened the metal clasp, and held it up to dump the contents. Angelica's curiosity got the best of her despite her ongoing trauma over the rat.

"What is it?" she asked as two rubber-banded stacks of board game money fell out. "Fake money? What's that all over it? Oh geez, tell me that isn't blood."

Sincerely hoping it was paint or ink, I grabbed a letter opener and scooted the play money back into the envelope. So not only did the killer know where I worked and the location of my office, but he also had managed to get a hold of an intracampus mailer. I called Jesse and left a message, telling him I'd be by after my last class and why. Maybe it was time to bow out. I was an unpaid consultant, a volunteer essentially, and had to ask myself if this was worth the fear and anxiety. Jesse had told me from the beginning that I could say I was out and there would be no hard feelings. It was tempting. To walk away and not have to think about a psychopath plotting his next gruesome play sounded like a fine plan.

But of course, I knew that even if I did tell Jesse I wanted to quit, I couldn't let go of the investigation that easily. The killer would still be out there, and until he was no longer a threat, I couldn't rest any more than Jesse could. I'd told him I was in for the long haul, and I'd meant it. I needed to see the investigation through to the end as much as he did. I was also determined to gather as much data as I could for my research paper. This was an absolute once-in-lifetime opportunity. And finally, call it ego, pride, or pure bullheaded stubbornness, but I bristled at the idea of letting the killer intimidate me. And yes, I know how dangerously ridiculous that sounds given that the one so intent on intimidating me was in fact a cold-blooded psychopathic serial killer. I mentally dug my heels in and thought I could hang on just a bit longer. That was easy to think sitting in my office surrounded by colleagues and with campus security a phone call away. But looking back, I still marvel at how easily I was able to quiet the inner voice of reason.

I left right after my last class and drove over to the police station. I'd put the campus mailer in a plastic grocery bag after phoning

Jesse. When he came to get me in the lobby, he took it from me without a word, and we went to the conference room.

"All mail sent within the campus is supposed to be in one of these?"

"Yeah, that's right."

"Would our guy have to go to the…what is it, the campus post office?"

"It's mail services in the Facilities Management building, which is actually near the main campus entrance. I guess he could've just walked in there and found one. But those envelopes aren't all that hard to come by. He could probably find one in the library or almost any other building."

"I really don't like how much time this asshole is spending at the university."

"Yeah, I don't like it much either. Although I kind of applaud the variety of ways he's sending me his nasty little gifts."

Jesse shook his head.

"Hey, if I don't keep making jokes, I'll crack."

"I get that. I'll have this stuff sent to the lab just in case they can find a latent print. Thanks for bringing it by."

We sat in silence for a moment, and then he said, "Ashley, you'd tell me if you wanted out of the investigation, wouldn't you?"

Did he sense the internal dialogue I'd had just a few hours ago?

"I would, Jesse, I swear. But I don't want out. This stuff," I said, pointing at the grocery bag, "is completely freaking me out. Believe me, it's doing its intended job, but I still think we're going to catch up with this creep. He's stepping up his game, and each time he does, there's more opportunity for him to slip up. He's going to get a little reckless in his pursuit of that bigger rush. And now he's got the added distraction of trying to intimidate me, and that's what this is about— intimidation. He's busy trying to prove to you guys how clever he is and I wasn't part of the plan, so he wants to scare me away."

Jesse leaned forward, forearms on the table, looked me in the eye intently, and said, "Do you still feel like you're not in any danger?"

"Physical danger? No. And maybe that's naive, but I don't. Psychological danger is more of a gray area, but this is my realm, and I still think we can beat this jerk at his own twisted game."

"That's admirable."

"It's probably more like ridiculously stubborn and hardheaded, but thank you."

He smiled. "Are you ready to get out of here? I'll follow you home."

"Be careful, I might get used to having my very own police escort."

"If I don't start making some headway with this case, that may become my new gig."

Talking to Jesse settled my nerves, and I successfully convinced us both that the killer was just out to intimidate me. I'm so good at deluding myself that I brought Jesse along for the ride. We walked outside, and I once again had the benefit of his seeing me safely home.

18

The next week was a short one due to the Thanksgiving holiday, leaving less time to grade papers and exams, plus I was behind on a book review I'd promised to write. I was also spending a lot more time with my grad students. As the end of the semester approaches, there tends to be a mad dash to complete research projects and write up the findings. As their adviser, my job is to offer encouragement and guidance, but the trick is to offer support without getting in the way or making being a perpetual student sound preferable to graduating and getting a job. On occasion, I've encountered students who do everything they can think of to stay within the safe confines of the university rather than going "out there," including changing minors, declaring a double major, and getting caught in the post-graduate cycle of thinking one more class will give them the edge they need to land the perfect job. I can't really blame them, as I experienced those same doubts about post-university life. And then, as fate would have it, I ended up back at my alma mater.

Papers critiqued and exams graded, I was about to go find something edible in the cafeteria before starting on the book review when Lydia knocked on my open door.

"Hi, Ashley, do you have a moment?"

As if saying no were an option.

"Of course, what's up?" I said, gesturing to the chair in front of my desk.

"Well, I wanted to talk to you about possibly heading up the Freshman Outreach Committee next semester."

Most people would be amazed to discover how little time college professors actually spend in the classroom and developing curriculum. A huge chunk of our time is spent doing research, writing and publishing papers and book reviews, advising students, and sitting on various committees. I was already part of two and didn't really relish the idea of taking on a third, let alone heading it.

"Oh well…uh…," I said. I'm quite articulate when stalling for time.

"I think you'd be a perfect fit. Your students love you and I've heard freshmen say how easy they think you are to talk to."

All in all, Lydia is a good boss, but she can lay it on a little thick at times.

"Well, that's awfully nice to hear. Can I think about it for a day or so and let you know?"

"Of course. I was just thinking that since you'll only be teaching three classes in the spring, you'll have the extra time."

Which meant it was already decided. Awesome.

"Ah, good point. I'll let you know for sure tomorrow, but I don't really see any reason why I'd say no."

She was good. I had to give her props.

"Excellent. I'll talk to you tomorrow," she said, getting up to leave. She paused in the doorway. "Ashley, I really have heard students say that you're easy to talk to. It's your empathy. They can feel it when they first meet you."

She walked away rather than staying to see my reaction. That's how Lydia delivers compliments: on the run, which is still better than not handing them out at all. I had to smile.

Wednesday night, I walked out to the parking garage with Tony, whose office is across the hall from mine. Tony's been at the university for twenty years, and one of the many things I like about him is his refusal to talk about work once he's walked out of the building. If you ask how his day went or how his classes were, you'll get a one-word answer. I spent most of my first semester on campus thinking he didn't like me and had no interest in talking to me. Then I asked about his weekend plans one day in the faculty dining room, and he talked my ear off. I'm aware that college professors are a quirky bunch, and I'm okay with fitting right in. We chatted about nothing of consequence on the way to our cars and then wished each other Happy Thanksgiving.

I started my car and was about to back out of the slot when I realized there was a flyer under the windshield wiper. I hate those things and thought that administration had ruled the faculty garage off limits for that kind of annoying advertising. I opened the door and grabbed it, discovering it was a postcard with a little sample vial of perfume stuck to it, like the ones they try to foist upon you in department stores. This one didn't list any stores, so whoever created the campaign did a lousy job, which made it even more annoying. I dropped it into my bag, intending to toss it when I got home and thinking it was likely a waste of time to ask administration if there wasn't something they could do to stop that kind of nonsense. I turned onto J Street and headed for home, bummed that it was already too dark to go to McKinley. Cody would have to settle for a quick walk around the block and maybe a few rounds of tossing a ball in the backyard.

I pulled into my driveway and saw my next-door neighbors and the couple from across the street standing on the sidewalk, chatting. I put the car in the garage and went out to say hello to everyone.

"I'm glad you're home, Ashley," said my across-the-street neighbor, Greg. "We've been talking about starting a neighborhood watch group."

No. Not my neighborhood, not my street, not my house. He can't be here...

"—if you'd like to be a part of it," said Linda, Greg's wife.

"Oh, um, sure, why not," I said, hoping she hadn't noticed that I'd missed most of whatever it was she'd just said. I concentrated on breathing and listening.

Samantha, who lives next door, said, "It just seems like a good idea given the state of the world in general but specifically what's been going on right here in Sacramento recently. This is still a great neighborhood, but that's even more reason to get something in place now, right?"

"Absolutely," Greg answered.

Samantha's partner, Monique, said, "I've already found out where we can order signs and window stickers."

"Keeping an eye on each other's houses and paying attention to who's coming and going is all well and good, and we need to keep it up. This is just the next step," said Linda.

"Right," said Monique. "Ellen told me this morning that she thought someone was in her backyard a few nights ago. Granted, she is a bit of an alarmist, but it wouldn't hurt to be extra vigilant, at least until the cops find this creep."

Someone in Ellen's backyard? Or Monique's? Or mine? The idea of the killer cruising through my neighborhood as casually as he was apparently roaming around on campus was like a kick to the stomach. I was aware of the possibility that he'd find out where I live, but so far, I'd been able to avoid thinking about it. The idea of him here, walking past my neighbors' houses, made me break out in a cold sweat.

"Yeah, great idea," I said, wondering if she'd noticed how many times Jesse had followed me home recently. Fortunately, we don't have a neighborhood gossip on our street. "Count me in and let me know what I can do."

"Excellent, I knew we could depend on you," said Samantha.

"Thanks, Ashley. This is how the good guys win," said Greg. I thought Jesse would agree. I wished everyone a happy Thanksgiving and went inside, desperately hoping that somehow the killer had not searched for my address. A neighborhood watch program was a fine idea, of course, but I didn't want to be the reason we suddenly needed one.

Cody greeted me with his usual energy and enthusiasm and herded me into the backyard, and we spent a good twenty minutes tossing a ball around. I hoped he'd get enough exercise to tire without going for a walk, even a short one around the block. I was too rattled to leave the yard. I watched him race after the ball each time I threw it with that single-minded determination border collies are known for. Such a graceful simplicity. Throwing the ball and having it returned to me was a meditative act that was enough to calm me down. When Cody lost interest in chasing the ball, which meant he was hungry, we went inside, and I gave him a larger-than-usual dinner, feeling guilty about skipping our walk. I then went around the house, checking and double-checking that all the doors and windows were secure.

Thanksgiving weekend came and went, the weather cooled significantly, and the end of the semester was in sight. I enjoyed a nice holiday dinner in the foothills with my parents and my older brother and his family, who had made the trip up from Southern California. My younger brother and sister-in-law spent the holiday in Oregon with her family. Cait came into town Wednesday afternoon, spent Thursday and Friday with her parents, and then arrived at my place Saturday night. I know her well enough to realize that I need to leave her be when she's in the middle of a story. She'd come back into town for Thanksgiving, but she was also chasing a lead. The Vegas plot had thickened considerably. It now appeared that the feds had enough evidence to pursue money laundering charges against the casino owner, but it also looked like his connection to West Sac was tied to Your Dream Ride somehow.

That, of course, looked awfully bad for Daniel. Cait was determined to keep digging into whatever was going on with him and refused to believe he could have anything to do with the chop shops or the guy in Vegas. There was also Daniel's partner's accusation that Daniel had emptied the corporate bank account. Since Cait still hadn't been able to reach him, she hadn't yet been able to hear his side of the story or find out if he even knew what Evan was claiming. I tried to imagine what she must have been feeling and how frustrating it would be not to be able to talk to someone I cared so much about when damaging accusations were stacking up. I also thought about what it must be like to confront the possibility of someone I was so close to committing a crime. Would I go straight to denial? Probably. Lose my objectivity? Most likely. Cait didn't need more questions right now; she needed a friend. And I'm deeply sorry to have to admit that I let her down.

19

He sipped his tea and waited for the Other to send him a vision. His next event needed to be different yet again. According to the latest report he saw on cable news, the cops had a working theory that his events might all have been the work of one person. Such simpletons…he could draw them a map and they'd still be wandering around bumping into each other. He had no trouble choosing a subject this time. Yes, this one absolutely needed a lesson on how to treat him. She was such a hothead, always going off and yelling about something; perhaps a cooldown was in order. He giggled and felt the rush of a plan beginning to take shape.

Of course, he also had the so-called expert to think about, the college professor who was working with the cops. If the professor was so smart, why hadn't she and the cops figured everything out yet? That one would have to be dealt with, too, in an incredibly special way. There was so much to do…he needed to get busy. But he'd learned that he needed a solid plan first. The Other had taught him that poorly thought-out plans lead to mistakes, and mistakes could lead to…best not to think about that. Oh! He'd just thought of the perfect way to show the smarty-pants professor that he was the smart one. He giggled again. The sun would be up soon. It was time to get ready to go to work and pretend to be a normal.

*****

After thinking about it all day, I decided on the way home that no matter how uncomfortable it might be, it was time to confront

Cait about what was going on with Daniel and what she was becoming increasingly entangled with. After wanting to talk about it almost constantly, she'd become nearly silent on the matter, just saying that she was "working on it." I was used to Cait in work mode, but this was different; since coming back into town last week, she was almost withdrawn, retreating to the guest room after dinner instead of sitting and chatting or watching a movie, saying that she had calls to make or research to do online. She'd texted earlier that she'd be out well past dinnertime and I should eat without her. Cait will pursue a story with a single-minded determination that is hugely impressive. While I didn't think she'd ever knowingly endanger herself, I was concerned that her drive to discover the truth, not to mention her feelings for Daniel, was clouding her judgment and that she might end up in real trouble.

Granted, I was jumpy since realizing the killer knew where I work and was likely close to figuring out where I live—if he hadn't already—but I wanted her to consider letting her investigation go. She really had no way of knowing what kind of people Daniel might be involved with and what they'd do to protect their interests. If Casino Guy's activities really were tied to Your Dream Ride, what did that mean for Daniel? What would happen if she were in too deep with a crooked casino owner with lord knows what kind of dangerous contacts? I had just filled the teakettle and set it on the stove when she came in the front door. Cody ran to greet her and then herded her into the kitchen.

"You read my mind. I was just thinking about having a cup of tea," she said.

Interesting choice of words since I'd spent the last few days wondering what she'd been thinking. I put two mugs and a tin of chamomile tea on the counter, and we sat down at the kitchen table to wait for the water to boil. *Quit stalling*, I told myself. Sometimes fearing conflict is a pain in the butt.

"I'm just going to jump in and say this—I'm worried about you, Cait."

"You're worried about me? I'm not the one who has some deranged psycho sending her dead rodents in the mail."

"That's a valid point, but you're involved in a pretty intense situation of your own, don't you think?"

She sighed. "I know this is looking bad for Daniel the further I dig into it, but I'm more convinced than ever that he's being set up. And if he's left to take the fall, he could end up going to prison. Prison, Ash. If that happened and I didn't do everything I could to expose the truth, I'd never forgive myself."

The kettle started to whistle, and I got up and turned off the burner. I was aware that I was stalling again, slowing pouring the water through the infusers and watching the herbs steep, but I was trying to collect my thoughts. I know Cait well enough to be sure my gut feeling that she was in danger wouldn't be enough to sway her. I also had to tread lightly and not make it sound like I thought Daniel might be guilty, even though I was becoming more convinced of that every time she gave me an update. I set a mug in front of her and sat down again.

"Look, I don't want to cast stones here. I'm involved in a high-profile murder investigation, and it's clear that the killer knows where I work. I know Daniel would never knowingly put you in harm's way, but you can't know anything about the people he's involved with."

"I know you mean well and I really do appreciate your concern, but I know what I'm doing. I've been an embedded reporter. I've been in the middle of a civil war."

"Yes, you have. You've done things that scare the hell out of me just thinking about them. But isn't this different?"

"It is unlike anything else I've done, yes, but I swear to you that I'm getting closer to figuring everything out. I've been talking to someone who knows about the entire operation, from when the cars are taken from the port to when the legitimate funds are funneled back into the casino. He might even be able to clear Daniel if I can get him to go on the record."

"Really? Who?"

"I can't tell you. I can't even risk telling Daniel I've been talking to this guy because he might bolt."

"You have a confidential source?"

"Yes, and I swore that I won't give him up even if this thing were to go to trial."

"Wouldn't you get charged with contempt if you did that?" I asked.

"And fined, or possibly even face jail time myself."

"Wait a minute, what? You'd go to jail over this guy?"

"If I had to. I can't very well promise not to give him up and then turn around and out him. My reputation would be shot. I'd be lucky to land a gig with a tabloid after that."

"Okay, so having this source is good for the story, but what about you? This guy in Vegas could have ties to the mob for god's sake. You're investigating people who are likely completely amoral and will do anything to protect their operations."

"Like I said, I appreciate your concern, but I know what I'm doing. This isn't your world, but it *is* mine. It's not like university politics, okay?"

I ignored the university jab and said, "I'm just saying you have an emotional stake in this story because of Daniel, and that might be clouding your thinking. You really have no way of knowing what you've gotten involved with, and your feelings for Daniel are in the way. Your judgment may be a bit off here."

I wasn't sure if I saw anger, hurt, or both in her eyes. "I assure you there is *nothing* wrong with my judgment," she said.

"Okay, but just because I don't live in your realm it doesn't mean I'm completely isolated at the university. I do pay attention to what's happening out here in the 'real' world. I'm not sequestered in my ivory tower."

"No, you're not. Sac State doesn't have ivory towers."

"Oh, so I'm just a prof at a Podunk state school?"

She shrugged. "It's not exactly the Ivy League."

It was a lousy thing to say but not untrue. I decided to let it go for the time being and try a different angle. "Have you considered that your blind loyalty to Daniel is keeping you from thinking this through all the way?"

"Blind loyalty isn't always a bad thing, Ash. There are some things you just have to take on faith. Maybe if you knew how to do that, things would have worked out differently for you and Jonathan."

That caught me by surprise, and it completely pissed me off. "Seriously? We're dredging up ancient history now? If anything, I had too much loyalty to Jonathan. Every time he doubted himself and wondered if he really had what it took to make it, I was the one who reassured him that he did. I was the one who told him to keep writing songs and get serious about learning the business side of a musical career while he was busy playing rock star and chasing groupies. But maybe you don't remember that part."

"I'm just saying that loyalty goes a long way in a relationship."

"And you think I'm alone because I don't get that?"

"That's not what I meant, and you know it."

"Then what did you mean?" Aware it was my temper speaking but unable to stop it, I went on. "You know, I'm not sure that someone whose relationship is off more than it's on is qualified to give advice. And if you seriously think you can go after a Vegas casino owner involved with god knows what kind of illegal activities, then you might need to check in with your objectivity *and* your judgment."

She stared at me. She was either silently counting to ten or ready to hit me with a brutal comeback. "I...I think we should pick this conversation up later. Good night." She put her mug in the sink and went down the hall to the guest room. I sat and sipped my tea. Over the years, I'd seen Cait come close to losing her temper when pushed. But this was the first time I'd been the one doing the pushing, and I didn't at all like how it felt. And now I needed to figure out how I was going to deal with insulting one of my oldest and dearest friends. While I do believe that most situations have something of value to teach us, I couldn't fathom what the lesson in all of this might be.

After tossing and turning all night, I managed to sleep through my alarm, waking up only when Cody started whining to go outside. Crap. I'd not only have to skip my morning workout but also have to hustle to make it to my eight-o'clock class on time. The door to the guest room was closed when I walked by to let the dog out, and I hoped Cait had gotten a better night's sleep than I had. Cody ran out, and looking out the side kitchen window, I saw that Cait's Audi was gone. I didn't think she'd just take off and go back to San Francisco without telling me, but our argument last night was new territory for us, and feeling as badly as I did about leaving it unresolved, I couldn't ignore that possibility. Cody came back in for his breakfast, and I went to take a quick shower and get myself ready for work. It would be poor form to be late after lecturing my freshmen about making a commitment to get to class on time no matter how early it starts.

In the middle of my afternoon office hour, Lydia stopped by.

"Do you have a minute, Ashley?"

"Of course," I said, gesturing to the chair in front of my desk. "What's on your mind?"

"It seems that one of your students, Kyle Reynolds, is upset about a grade."

How could she possibly know about that? "He did come to talk to me about a D—which he earned—on one test. I told him it was nothing to freak out over and that he has plenty of time to bring his grade up."

She hesitated. "Apparently, that didn't reassure him. He went to the dean, accusing you of being unfair and targeting him because you don't like him."

That, a first in twenty years of teaching, left me speechless. I stared at her.

"Ashley, I know you and I know how you treat your students. I don't believe for a minute that you're treating Kyle any differently than any of the others. Unfortunately, all complaints received by the dean's office have to be investigated."

I found my voice. "*Investigated?* What does that mean?"

"Don't worry," she said, holding up a hand, "it just means we need to look into the matter, starting with me talking to you like this. I'll talk to Kyle next, and that will likely be the end of it."

"Likely?"

"You may need to speak with the dean, but if you do, just tell him what you told me. Your record speaks for itself, Ashley, and you really have nothing to worry about. If you teach long enough, you'll encounter a problem student. Most of us have at least one in our careers."

"Thanks for the heads-up," I said, "and your confidence."

She nodded and got up to leave and then stopped in the doorway. "Ashley, it wouldn't hurt to go see the dean before you're asked to. You haven't exactly made yourself visible. Think about what I said about learning to play the game a bit." She left before I could reply.

I sat staring at the empty doorway, suddenly too bone-weary to do anything else. What a week. A murderous psycho hell-bent on intimidating me is regularly strolling around campus, my efforts to help the cops find said psycho have so far turned up a big fat nothing, a disgruntled student went to the dean over a D on a test, the department chair is on my ass for not giving a damn about university politics, and my best friend isn't speaking to me. I knew better than to tempt fate and think it couldn't get any worse, but I had to wonder how on earth I'd gotten here. Whose life was this?

After a long day at the end of an exceedingly long week, I was in the backyard tossing a ball for Cody when I heard Cait pull into the driveway. She hadn't been in touch all day, but I didn't contact her either. Letting her be to work through whatever she's dealing with is generally what she wants. But what really kept me silent was my embarrassment at how I'd behaved last night. What kind of person hurls accusations at her best friend when she needs support more than anything? Cait and I had never been at odds apart from a few exhaustion-driven petty arguments during finals week in college. I felt like a lousy excuse for a friend, who'd let her down when she most needed me. The wind had picked up, so it was getting chilly. I told Cody we were done playing, and we walked into the kitchen at the same time as Cait.

She put a bottle of wine on the table and said, "Hey, I'm sorry I took off without saying anything this morning."

"I should be apologizing to you," I said. "I had no business questioning your judgment and no reason to say you shouldn't be pursuing your story. It's not my place to comment on what Daniel might be involved with, and I honestly don't doubt that you know what you're doing. I...I just let fear take over."

She came over and hugged me. "You were just letting me know how much you care, which I greatly appreciate. I was completely out of line bringing up Jonathan, and I'm sorry I made it sound like I think you're out of touch at the university because I don't."

And just like that, we were right again. The tension and weighty unease I'd carried all day melted away.

"How about I open this wine and we make a giant pot of spaghetti?" she said.

"Good wine and comfort food with my best friend on a Friday night? Count me in."

We made a big salad and far too much spaghetti, lingering over the meal, and then stayed up late finishing the wine and talking like we used to in our dorm days. One of the greatest things about Cait's job is her freedom to dictate her own hours, which allows her to breeze into and out of town on a whim. I've learned to have no expectations as to when I might see her and just appreciate what time we're able to spend together.

The following Tuesday morning should have been a late one, but I arrived on campus earlier than usual for a committee meeting. Angelica, a few of our colleagues, and I listened to a presentation from Tony, during which he spoke about finding and applying for available grants to fund research efforts at the university. College professors, especially those in the scientific fields, spend quite a bit of their time seeking out and applying for various grants. I dutifully typed notes on my laptop that I'd distribute to the committee members, department chair, and the dean. On the way back to our building, I saw that the sun had burned off the morning fog and the sky was a brilliant blue. I very much wanted the bright sunshine to be an omen of things to come. Too bad it wasn't.

Back in our office, I started gathering my notes for the pop culture class and realized Angelica was studying me.

"What?"

She hesitated. "I know you're not supposed to talk about the investigation, but…"

"I'm not. You know I can't tell you anything more than what you've already read about or seen on the news."

"That's not what I'm after. I just want to know if you're okay. I mean, all of this has got to be affecting you. If it were me, I'd be a giant ball of stress."

"It's stressing me out, believe me. I've learned things I never wanted to know about the depths of human cruelty. But Jesse arranged for me to talk to the department psychologist, and he and his partner are always available to talk to. I'm okay, but thanks."

There was clearly more on her mind. I waited.

"Okay, so much for your mental state, but are you sure you're still safe?" She glanced at the doorway. "A *killer* knows who you are and where you work. He's sent you creepy things in the mail and has obviously been here on campus. What if...how much harder would it be to figure out where you live?"

"I've thought of that, too, as have Jesse and Ed. At this point, we're convinced that the killer is toying with us, trying to show us how clever he is. And he's trying to intimidate me and scare me off. But I'm not part of the big picture. I'm just a minor annoyance." I was working extremely hard to keep believing that.

She didn't seem convinced but said, "Okay, if you say so. Sorry to harp on it, but this is still seriously freaking me out."

"No worries. There'd be something wrong with you if you weren't freaked out. And thanks. I have to get to class. Are you sitting in today?"

"I wish I could," she said, "but I've got essays to read. Can I assume that you're going to continue to sidestep Michael's request to discuss horror movies?"

"As long as I possibly can."

She smiled and gave me a thumbs-up as I headed out the door.

Michael persisted, and thanks to pressure from the class, I reluctantly gave in.

"So what is it about horror movies? And for the purposes of this discussion, let's focus on the classic Hitchcock-style horror flick, not the slasher movies that rely on fake blood and body parts to get the point across. Why do we like to be scared? Is it akin to riding a roller coaster, the anticipation of that drop we know is coming?"

Most of the class nodded their heads and agreed that the suspense of waiting for the drop was thrilling.

Michael raised his hand and said, "It's knowing something that the characters in the film don't. We know the guy in the abandoned house shouldn't go down the dark hallway, but he doesn't, so there he goes."

"It's sort of like reading a mystery," Debbie said. "I love it when I figure out what's going to happen before I get to the end."

"And why is that?" I asked.

She smiled. "It makes me feel clever. Once I discovered *Harriet the Spy* when I was a kid, I couldn't get enough."

"Then it's the thrill of waiting for the drop," I said, writing the word on the whiteboard, "plus the opportunity to feel intelligent that adds up to being entertained." I put the rest of the equation on the board.

$$Thrill + Clever = Fun$$

We spent the rest of the class discussing favorite scenes in classic horror movies like *Psycho* and novels like *The Shining* and why the genre was as popular as ever. Thinking in terms of fiction calmed my nerves a bit, and I was able to get through the class without undue anxiety.

After navigating bumper-to-bumper traffic, I walked into the station that evening with a knot in my stomach. When Jesse texted, asking me to come by, a deep sense of dread settled upon me. The killer was going on with his sick game while we were no closer to figuring out how to stop him. I checked in with the desk clerk, picked up my visitor pass, and waited for Jesse. When he and I went into the conference room, Detective Marquez was already at the table with the murder book. He looked at me over the top of his reading glasses, and I could see the frustration in his deep brown eyes. He went back to the report and started to fill me in on the latest gruesome discovery.

"A little after ten this morning, two cyclists on the bike trail found a woman at the edge of the river between the Watt and Howe

Avenue bridges. Her body was caught in vegetation at the shore. Cause of death has been ruled drowning, and the time of death is estimated as sometime between midnight and 2:00 a.m., though it may be later, as being in the river would cause her body temp to drop faster."

Jesse reached for the photos and spread them out on the table.

"It's possible this was an accident that has nothing to do with this investigation. If the woman fell into the river and drowned—and given the temperature of the water this time of year, it wouldn't take long for hypothermia to set in—she could have floated downstream until she got caught in the bushes. There's no scenario here, no calling card. If this is the work of our lunatic, why didn't he stage anything?"

I looked at the photos and felt an instant chill, shuddering and thinking of the poor woman taking a last desperate breath before succumbing to the icy water and going under. So much for clinical detachment. One of the shots was taken from a distance, showing the location of the body in relation to the bike trail, and I knew exactly where it was. How many times had I ridden past that exact spot? Detachment fail number two.

As I looked at the report, scanning the info Ed had just read through, a uniformed officer came into the room, apologized to the detectives for the interruption, and handed Ed a few sheets of paper. The supplemental information was written after a follow-up search of the area where the woman had been discovered. Relaying to us what he was reading, Detective Marquez said the search team did find some items at the scene.

"A green scarf was tangled in the bushes near where her body was found, and a little bottle of perfume was wrapped in one end of the scarf."

Jesse looked at me. "Any idea what that could mean?"

"None," I said, going back to the initial report I'd been reading. I came to the list of items found in the woman's pockets. Keys, lip balm, ID—"Oh no."

"What?" Jesse and Ed asked simultaneously.

"There was a daily CSUS parking permit in one of her pockets."

I was aware that my heart was pounding, and my anxiety level was rising. But it didn't last long; it soon morphed into sheer terror.

"Ed, does the report say if that scarf is green and gold, or if it has any kind of logo on it?" I asked.

"Let's see…yeah, it's got gold stripes and a green-and-gold double S. Why?"

Something with hundreds of icy feet crawled up my spine.

"Those are Sac State's colors. Does it say what kind of perfume?" I asked, barely above a whisper.

"Something called Poison. That's a dumb name for a perfume."

"Ashley, are you okay?" Jesse asked.

I shook my head, trying to breathe to calm myself as I felt tears well up. I had completely forgotten about the sample bottle of perfume left on my car two weeks ago.

I opened my mouth to speak but couldn't. I tried again. "Two weeks ago, I found a sample bottle of that perfume. It was attached to a postcard left on my windshield."

"What? Ashley, I thought we agreed that you'd let me know when something like that happened. Why didn't you tell me?!" Jesse shouted.

"Take it down a notch, partner," Ed cautioned.

"I thought it was just one of those promotions where they leave flyers on cars. I seriously forgot about it right after I tossed it. I would have mentioned it if I thought it was at all significant," I said as the tears started to fall.

"I'm sorry I raised my voice," Jesse said, putting his hand on my arm. "But that's it, you're off the case. You're done."

I couldn't say anything as I dug in my purse for a tissue.

"I'm so sorry, Ashley. I should never have dragged you into this."

"Jess is right. You're out, Ashley," Eduardo said gently.

I didn't have the strength to argue with them, plus I was more than a little rattled. It was certainly possible that the parking permit was a coincidence but not the scarf too. And the dead rat, board game money, and the Cure CD that showed up at my office were scary enough, but the killer was so intent on intimidating me that he staked out my car and left one of his sick clues on it. Our lunatic had become quite comfortable wandering around the campus and going into my building, and he had obviously been hanging around the parking garage as well. I made a weak argument that I could still offer advice and wouldn't come to the station anymore but didn't even succeed in convincing myself that I should still be a part of the investigation.

"Okay," I said, wiping my eyes, "I'm out. This is too much. For the record, I bet the clue here is the Beach Boys' 'Be True to Your School,' but I guess that doesn't matter, does it? We know what he's really saying…" Fresh tears ran down my cheeks.

Ed and Jesse were obviously beyond caring about my solving the riddle at that point.

"I'm going to follow you home right now," Jesse said. "When you get there, put your car into the garage right away, get inside, and set your alarm. Ed, can you assign a black and white to cruise the neighborhood and keep an eye on Ashley's house until this is over?"

Already on the phone, Ed nodded.

"What time will you get to work in the morning?" Jesse asked.

"Seven thirty. Monday, Wednesday, and Friday are my early days."

"I'll meet you there at seven tomorrow, and we'll talk to campus security."

I nodded. Speaking took too much effort, and I was using all of it to hold myself together. Then I thought of something.

"Jesse, what do I tell Cait? She's going to know something's up the minute she looks at me."

He took a deep breath, and I could see him struggle to control his emotions. He let out a heavy sigh.

"Tell her that Ed and I decided it was too dangerous for you to continue to be a part of this. How long is she staying with you?"

"She hasn't decided yet."

"As much as I don't like that it's my sister, I'm glad you're not going to be alone in your house."

"I've got good neighbors on either side of me, Cody is a great watchdog, and I always set the alarm at night."

"All good things, but I let you be involved in this for way too long. This should never have happened."

Ed had been watching Jesse with something akin to parental concern. "Beating yourself up won't get you anywhere, Detective. Focus on the task at hand and we'll deconstruct the case and any missteps later."

Jesse nodded and stood up. "Okay. Let's get going."

We went outside to see the fog already setting in, and I didn't think I could feel any colder. Ed told me the black and white would be in my neighborhood by the time I got home, said good night, and then got into his car and headed for Elk Grove. Jesse pulled out of the parking lot behind me, and I concentrated on his headlights in my rearview, telling myself I was safe for the moment. I drove home shivering despite turning the heat on full blast, white-knuckling the steering wheel. I was glad he was following me, but Jesse was going to leave after I went inside. The full realization of the potential danger I was in hit me like a freight train. What the hell had I been thinking, agreeing to get involved in a murder investigation? Why didn't I walk away after the dead rat? I could call Colleen in the morning, but what was I to do tonight?

Cait's car wasn't parked out front when we got to my house, and I sent a silent plea for her protection to the universe. The black and white patrol car rounded the corner onto my street as I turned into the driveway, and Jesse parked and went over to talk to the officers. I put the car in the garage and shut the door, going through the motions on autopilot. Jesse watched me approach my front door and called, "Ashley, call me if you need anything…or just to talk if you want."

"Thanks, Jesse, I will." I watched him get into his car, gave thanks for my amazing watchdog, and then went into my cold, dark home, hearing Jesse drive away. I reset the alarm and then walked around the house, turning on every light and checking every door and window twice, Cody at my heels. I was still shivering, so I bumped up the heat, changed into sweats, and made a cup of tea. Then Cody and I settled on the couch to wait for Cait.

She arrived about forty minutes later. Cody ran to greet her and herded her into the living room.

"Hey," she said, "I stopped by to check on my mom after I left the library—what's up? Are you okay? And why did you set the alarm so early?"

What did I tell Jesse? Cait reads me like no one else. "It's been quite a day. The killer struck again."

"Oh shit, really?" She sat down next to me.

"Yeah, another victim and we're no closer to finding this lunatic. But also…I'm off the case."

"You are? Why?"

"Jesse and Ed thought it was just too dangerous for me to continue, and I have to say I'm relieved."

"So they just decided you needed to bow out and that was that?"

"Yeah," I nodded.

"No other reason?"

"Nope."

She looked at me, and I knew she didn't buy my simple explanation but decided to let it rest for the moment.

"Well…it must feel good to have that weight off your shoulders."

I nodded.

"Hey, we should find some silly comedy to watch. What do you think?"

"That's a great idea," I said, grateful she decided not to press me on what was really going on.

"I'm going to change and make myself some tea. Find something that looks good," she said, handing me the remote. She returned a few minutes later, and we decided an old Monty Python special would do the trick. It did feel awfully good to laugh, especially sitting there with my two best friends. And how anyone could fail to laugh at the Python troupe's antics, especially John Cleese's Ministry of Silly Walks, is beyond me.

Over the next few days, the fog vanished, the weather warmed up a bit, and my mood shifted. Leaving the investigation had lifted a weight off my shoulders I wasn't aware had been so burdensome. The killer was still out there, likely planning his next horrible crime, but

I was doing my best to stay removed and leave the case to Jesse and Ed. I had convinced myself that the last scenario was orchestrated to scare me off since the gifts the killer sent hadn't. Cait had been spending as much time as she could with her mom, whose ankle was slowly healing, but came to hang out for the weekend. It was one of those early-December days that make me so happy to live in Sacramento. The sky was a perfectly clear blue, the air was clean, and the temperature would top out near fifty degrees.

After a lazy morning and a late breakfast of eggs, fruit, and homemade biscuits, Cait and I took Cody for a long, leisurely walk through my neighborhood, enjoying the quiet, the fresh air, and each other's company. We walked in silence for a few blocks, and then she said, "So you're off the case completely? You're not even talking to those guys anymore?"

I'd been wondering when she was going to circle back to that conversation.

"Not at all—I'm totally removed."

"Did that decision come from the higher-ups? Or Jesse and Ed?"

"Pretty much mutually Jesse and Ed. They were both worried about my safety, and the creepy gifts freaked them out almost as much as they did me."

"I can see why. You okay with being out? I mean, you're not frustrated that you don't get to see it through?"

Most people would be so frightened that a murderer knows my identity, where I work, and what I drive they wouldn't even think about being frustrated over not being a part of the resolution of the case. But then most people haven't been embedded in the middle of a civil war or hidden in a rebel base camp. Cait's CV is nothing short of extraordinary and still floors me when I stop to think about it. And while she's proud of her accomplishments, she also has a carefree "this is just what I do" attitude about her stellar career.

"I'm really not. It was fascinating to be involved, but I got way too close for comfort."

She reached over and touched my arm. "Yeah, you sure did. I'm glad...nothing happened."

"Thanks, friend. Me too."

Yesterday, I'd confirmed that Stephen's band was playing at Backstage Pass that evening, so we were planning to go.

"All right, tell me about this guy Stephen. You've been talking about him a lot lately."

"He's a friend who's in a band."

She gave me her "duh" look. "So you've said. I meant tell me about *him*. How did you meet, and more importantly, why does he make you smile when you say his name?"

I started to protest and realized she was right. I do smile when I talk about Stephen. And Cait of all people knows the signs of my being smitten. Dammit, busted.

"Okay, okay. I met him through friends. They invited me to an acoustic show he did at a charity benefit last year. We chatted afterward and discovered we have a lot in common, plus a fair amount of chemistry."

"And you're not dating because…"

I let out a big sigh. "Because he's at least eight years younger than me, he's incredibly busy with his day job, trying to keep the band going, and he's a *musician*."

"Seriously, girl? Don't you think it's time you let that go? Are you really going to let Jonathan affect the rest of your freaking life?"

I had neither a witty comeback nor a legitimate answer for that, so I just shrugged. Cait was the one person who knew the whole story of what transpired between Jonathan and me all those years ago and why I swore I'd never date another musician.

"Some rules are meant to be broken, Ash. Think about it."

We were back on my street by then. She was right, of course, but as any psychologist will tell you, giving advice is much easier than taking it to heart.

Jonathan…where to begin? We met early in my senior year at a mutual friend's party and hit it off immediately. As most local musicians did, he hung out at Tower, always showing up when I was working. We spent many a late-night closing shift chatting and flirting. He was talented, driven, charismatic, and gorgeous with big deep brown eyes and a killer smile. I told myself I needed to concentrate on school and didn't have time to date, but he pursued me relentlessly, wrote songs about me, and I fell for him. Hard. Music and everything that went with it, his world, was so enticing in contrast to academia. I spent every moment I could with him and thought nothing of staying out at a club until closing time and then tiptoeing into my dorm room, trying not to wake Cait.

His band, Velocity, started playing in San Francisco and Los Angeles and getting more shows in bigger venues while they pursued the Holy Grail—a contract with a record label. Once I started grad school, I had more academic demands and a lot more homework but still managed to be the supportive girlfriend, listening to ideas for new songs and sympathizing with Jonathan over tensions within the band and the frustrations of the elusive label contract. I'd made the move to Tower's main office in West Sacramento by then, the bump in pay allowing me to move out of the dorms and rent a small duplex not far from downtown. I worked during the day and then raced to the university to make it to evening classes. Velocity had pooled their resources to record a professional demo, and I gave a copy to every record label rep who walked into the advertising department. I don't know if it was my efforts, Jonathan's determination, or the combination, but Velocity got their contract with Atlantic, one of Warner's many labels, and recorded an album.

The band went on tour in support of that album, opening for Matchbox Twenty throughout the United States. I went to shows when I could but had precious little spare time between work, school, and finishing my thesis. Jonathan jumped into the rock star role wholeheartedly, loving every minute of it. I knew that he especially appreciated the female attention, and why shouldn't he? Even Paul McCartney admits that he and John Lennon wanted to be in a band to "pull birds." An indisputable fact, groupies are part of the scene, and great-looking, charismatic lead singers will never go without. But Jonathan assured me that reveling in the attention of female fans was all part of the act, and I believed him when he told me he was faithful. Silly me. Shortly after the tour ended, the label made plans for the band to record a follow-up album after a brief European tour.

I'd been in denial about how much we'd drifted apart while our primary focuses were pulling us in such different directions. Sitting across from Jonathan at a café the night he told me about the upcoming tour, I felt like I was looking at a stranger. It was devastating. I realized he felt the same way as he looked at me with those beautiful eyes and said, "I've missed you, Ash. What happened to us?" He then invited me to go to Europe with him. I hesitated, and he pleaded. "Come with me, please," he said, taking my hand in both of his. "We can get back to what we were—we just need to be together." The timing worked out, as the tour wouldn't start until after I was due to present my thesis. And taking a break before jumping into my doctoral studies sounded like a fabulous idea. So I applied for a rush passport, quit my job, and flew to London with my rock star boyfriend.

The fairy tale lasted for a few blissful weeks, and then it became clear that Jonathan was a bit of a Jekyll and Hyde on the road, wanting to appear single one minute and then wanting me in the spotlight with him, telling the audience which songs he'd written for me, his muse, the next. It was exhilarating, confusing, and exhausting all at once. I chose not to see the signs and tried not to crowd him when he wanted time apart. I ignored what my gut was telling me and concentrated on enjoying being in England. When we did spend his off time together, we played tourist, crossing must-see items off our list, and took an afternoon to go by Abbey Road Studios and take photos of ourselves on the iconic crosswalk. Watching him perform, I was struck by how incredibly good he and the band had become by playing night after night. It was a thrill to see their hard work and dedication pay off.

Cait had left school after graduating with her bachelor's degree and was enjoying well-earned success as a highly respected journalist. She joined me in Paris, and we hung out for a few days sightseeing and reconnecting. Her life sounded so exotic and exciting compared to what was waiting for me in California. Even back then though, I knew I wanted more out of my life than following the band and waiting in the wings while Jonathan was on stage. They were scheduled to go to Germany next, but as it turned out, I didn't go with them. After spending Cait's last day in the city with her, I returned to the hotel to find Jonathan with a young Parisian Goth girl who looked barely eighteen. She simply got out of bed and took her time getting dressed, eyeing me as if my sudden appearance were no big deal. Then she blew Jonathan a kiss and sauntered out the door.

He leapt up, hurriedly putting on his jeans, and stammering about how the girl meant nothing. He watched me hastily pack, not caring how I tossed my clothes and toiletries into the suitcase. He begged me to stay, to give him another chance, but didn't even try to tell me that I'd just walked in on his one and only indiscretion. He went on about the pressures of the tour, what it was like to have girls screaming at him every night, and how men can be weak. He said a lot of things, but notably missing were the words, "I'm sorry." My suitcase packed, I paused with my hand on the door.

"Say something, Ash, anything."

I finally looked at him and just said, "Goodbye, Jon."

Then I took a taxi to the airport and flew home, vowing never to date another musician. I didn't cry until somewhere over the Atlantic, staring out the window at the darkness, my haunted, tear-stained reflection looking back at me.

*****

Cait and I parked down the block from the club and were walking toward it when I saw Frank hanging around outside. Really? There hadn't already been enough weirdness in the week? I was hoping to sneak in unnoticed, but no such luck.

"Hey, Ashley, how are you? You here to see Evolution Theory?"

"Hi, Frank. Yeah, we're just on our way in."

He looked at Cait, and I would've felt like a complete jerk if I didn't introduce them, so I did the perfunctory, "Cait, meet Frank. Frank, this is Cait."

She had obviously picked up on Frank's odd vibe and raised her eyebrows. I told Frank we were meeting friends inside, and we made a hasty retreat.

"He's…interesting," she said.

"Yeah, isn't he? Sorry about that. Frank used to sell new releases to me at Tower when he worked for Sony. I had no idea he was back in the area until a few weeks ago when I ran into him downtown."

"Has he always been so—"

"Yep."

We went into the club and saw that the band was still setting up. I was about to suggest grabbing a table when Stephen saw us and came over.

"Hey, our super fan is here!"

"Hi, Stephen, good to see you."

We hugged and he kissed my cheek. I introduced Cait, and we spent a few minutes chatting. He said he needed to finish setting up, so he went back to the stage as we found a table.

"You've been holding out on me. He's freakin' adorable," Cait said.

"Yeah, he is, and guess what? At least half the women in town agree with you."

"You really need to chill. What are you drinking tonight, zin? Petite Sirah?"

"Surprise me," I said as she headed toward the bar.

Ian's partner, Jeff, came by as Cait returned to the table with our wine.

"You're Ian's friend, right?"

I complimented his memory and introduced Cait.

"Well, you shouldn't be too impressed since I can't remember your name," he confessed.

I reminded him and asked about Ian, and he told us his partner had taken a rare day off after working the last several in a row.

"Good for him," I said. "Looks like a pretty good crowd tonight."

He nodded, looking around the room. "Yeah, I just may ask these guys if they'd like to be the house band."

Cait asked how long the club had been open, and Jeff gave her the brief history and then said he wanted to check in with the guys at the door before the show started.

"Good to see you again, Ashley, and nice meeting you, Cait. Enjoy the show, and I'm sure I'll be back by at some point."

Looking around the room, Cait said, "This place is great, but I couldn't begin to handle the stress of running a club. Can you imagine worrying about the bar and the wait staff and wondering if the band is going to bring in a crowd or if someone will get drunk and get in a fight?"

This from a woman who thinks nothing of jumping on a plane to the Middle East with a day's notice. Personality variations will never cease to fascinate me. One person's adventure is another's nightmare.

"To those of us lucky enough to find our niche," I said, raising my glass.

She touched hers to mine. "Amen to that."

Evolution Theory is one of those bands that are difficult to categorize. They could be alternative rock or contemporary, or even alternative country. Stephen and Jason are the principal songwriters and share lead vocals. They do a few covers but mostly original material. The crowd quieted as the band came on stage. They opened with one of their original tunes, which was met with cheers and applause. Cait grabbed my arm. "Wow, they're really good!"

"I knew you'd think so."

It was good to see her relax and enjoy the music. Whatever was going on with Daniel still had Cait seriously upset, and I still wasn't convinced that she could stay out of trouble.

Stephen came over to sit with us during the break between sets, and I couldn't help but get caught up in his enthusiasm, not to mention his charm. He loves performing and is so at home on stage he makes it look effortless. He wanted to know what we thought of the show, of course, and then went on to tell us that he and Jason were busy writing songs for their next album. It occurred to me that Evolution Theory represents a new class of musician: those who are every bit as talented and driven as the pros but know they aren't likely to get that one-in-a-million lucky break, so they keep their day jobs and fit writing, rehearsing, recording, and performing into their schedules as best they can. Jason signaled to Stephen that the next set was about to start, so he touched his glass to ours and went back to the stage.

Cait caught me watching him walk away.

"Oh, you've got it bad…but so does he."

"What? What are you taking about?"

"Come on, he's totally flirting. What's wrong with you? How blind can you be?"

"He's sweet and friendly. I'm sure he talks to a lot of women like that. Plus, he's on right now, so he's extra animated."

She shook her head. "Look, I know you don't want to get hurt again and I get that, but you and Joe broke up, what, three years ago? It's time to open your heart, Ash. Don't ignore what's right in front of you because you're too scared to see if there's something there."

I had nothing to say to that and fortunately didn't have to say anything because the music started as the band began their second set.

Cait and I hung out after the show, chatting with Stephen and Jason as they broke down and loaded their gear. She asked Jason about the band's origin and how long he'd been playing and writing music. Cait is naturally warm and outgoing and genuinely enjoys talking to people. And while I knew she was legitimately interested in what Jason was saying, I also knew what she was up to. The only way it could be more obvious that she was trying to give Stephen and me an opportunity to talk would be if she were to pull Jason away on some flimsy pretext. He was playing it cool, but Jason was obviously enjoying chatting with her. He had most certainly noticed her when we first arrived. Introvert that I am, I'm fine with Cait being the one to capture attention wherever we go.

20

The first thing I did when I got into my office was call Colleen to set up an appointment. The clues at the last crime scene had done their job and then some: I was completely freaked out. A serial killer knew my identity, where I work, and recognized my car. What was to stop him from figuring out where I live? If he hadn't already done so, that is. And as much as I applauded my neighbors for their organized watch activities, I didn't feel any safer. I kept telling myself that the killer sent the items to intimidate me and, as a warning, to get me to stop consulting with the detectives, which I had. The perfume on my car, not to mention the Sac State scarf and parking permit, had put me over the edge. I was still kicking myself for dismissing the perfume at the time, but it bothered Jesse and Ed even more and marked the official end of my involvement in the case.

I hadn't been to the station or met Jesse at the café in nearly three weeks. The trouble, of course, was that there wasn't exactly a way to announce that to the public and, thus, the killer since my involvement had never been announced in the first place. Jesse asked me if I'd consider taking a leave of absence until the case wrapped up, but I couldn't see doing that with so little time left in the semester and wasn't sure what that would accomplish. And scarily enough, there was no telling how long it would take to solve the deadliest case the capital city had seen in more than thirty years, which I suppose isn't all that long when considering something so horrific.

In the 1980s, a woman named Dorothea Puente ran a boarding house in downtown Sacramento. She murdered her tenants, many of whom were elderly or mentally disabled, and buried them in her backyard. She then cashed their Social Security checks. She was responsible for nine confirmed deaths and suspected of another six that were never verified. After being questioned about a missing homeless man she'd taken in, she was arrested and convicted in 1988 and spent the rest of her life in a women's prison in Chowchilla. Shortly after the case broke, a local author wrote a book, laying out the gruesome details of the murders that had taken place between 1982 and 1988 and the bodies that were buried in the backyard of the Victorian house on F Street.

An industrious soul cashed in on the case, selling T-shirts with a cartoon likeness of the "death house landlady" in front of her Victorian, holding a shovel complete with notches in the handle and the slogan, "I Dig F Street." I was working at the record store then, and our neighboring bookstore sold quite a few of the books and a lot of shirts—mostly to Tower employees. It's human nature to turn to humor in the face of tragedy to help us cope. But there's also a fascination with the sinister, and when something so disturbing happens so close to home, we unconsciously need to be a part of it, at least as observers. I listened to coworkers and customers alike telling me about walking by the house on their way to catch the bus or living just around the corner. One regular customer who worked swing shift at a local radio station swore that he saw a guy in dirty coveralls standing on the sidewalk in front of the boarding house as he drove home late one night after work.

Jesse called while I was in my office reading student papers from my contemporary issues class. I was a bit surprised to hear from him. We hadn't been in touch since I ended my involvement with the investigation. We said our hellos, and I thought I heard more than fatigue in his voice. He asked if I was going to be in the office for a while and if he might come by to see me. Wondering what was so important that it needed to be shared immediately and in person, I told him I didn't have a class until four o'clock. I reminded him where to get a visitor parking permit and how to find Amador Hall, and he said he was on his way.

Detective Malone showed up just after Angelica left for class. The strain I'd heard in his voice was nothing compared to what I saw on his face. I invited him to have a seat and put a bottle of water on the desk in front of him.

"Thanks. How have you been?"

"I'm okay. How about you? What's going on?"

He sighed. "I'm off the case."

"What? Why?"

"The captain decided it would be better for me to focus my energies on something with a 'lower profile.' She thought it was completely reckless of me to get a private citizen involved to the extent that I did." He looked at the floor, as if eye contact cost him a bit too much. "She kind of freaked out when she found out about all the stuff the killer sent you."

"But I agreed to get involved. I knew we were talking about a potential serial killer. Okay, so I didn't know he'd find out who I am and be so comfortable strolling around campus, but I knew we were dealing with a psychopath."

"Doesn't matter, it's still on me."

He sounded so defeated it nearly made me cry.

"I'm sorry, Jesse. They didn't—you're not suspended, are you?"

"No, not yet, anyway, and I'm sure I have Ed to thank for that. He really went to bat for me. And you know, maybe this is for the best. The investigation was really starting to wear me down."

He leaned forward with an elbow on the desk and rubbed his eyes. I didn't know what to say. Jesse had been working the investigation since August, and now it was early December.

"Is Ed still working on it?"

"Yeah, he and another detective who has a lot of time in grade, Lisa Choe."

"So what are you doing?"

"Besides waiting to see if I'll have a suspension hearing? Not much more than paperwork, but hey, in my line of work, no customers is a good thing, right?" He attempted a weak smile.

My heart sank. Here was one of the sincerest people I'd ever met, a guy who chose a career in which he'd regularly put himself in dangerous situations in the name of helping the good guys, and he'd been asked to walk away from the most intense and involved case he was ever likely to see. Sometimes the lack of fairness in the universe is just too much to deal with.

"Well, I'll let you get back to what you were doing," Jesse said.

He stood and offered his hand. I felt like I should hug him instead but settled for the handshake.

"Take care of yourself, Ash. Call Ed if you get any more strange things sent here. We'll still have a patrol car in your neighborhood as long as this guy is running free, okay?"

I nodded. "Thanks."

"You can call me too… I mean if you want to talk…"

"Thanks, Jesse, I appreciate that. I'll walk out with you. I could use a sky break."

At the moment, it didn't occur to me that being seen with Jesse might not be the best thing for either of us. Chalk up another point for hindsight.

I'd arranged to see Colleen the next day after my morning office hour and left campus shortly past ten. She greeted me with her usual warmth and ushered me into her office. Her outfit was elegantly understated: a light gray cashmere sweater over a charcoal gray pencil skirt with a fuchsia scarf for a splash of color. I could learn a thing or two about fashion from her. I wondered if she'd consider going clothes shopping with me. I'd planned to ask her if she'd spoken to Jesse recently and if she knew he'd been removed from the case, but once she asked how I was doing, everything just poured out, starting with the latest creepy gifts and walking around campus wondering if the killer was watching me and ending with the latest murder and clues that pointed at me.

"You're tougher than I am," she said. "I'd have walked after the rat."

"You're smarter than I am. I tried to convince Jesse that it could have come from someone other than the killer. Students have pulled similar pranks. Not on me, but one of the Econ professors found a dead snake in his office last year."

"Seriously? Did he find out which student was responsible?"

"No. He had his suspicions but decided to let it go."

She shook her head. "And I thought police work was tough. All kidding aside, though, how are you feeling about all of this now that you're no longer part of the investigation? And after…those last clues? You obviously know the symptoms of acute stress, but we don't always recognize them in ourselves, especially those of us in this profession. Are you having trouble sleeping or concentrating?"

I shook my head. "No, but I do still think about the investigation pretty much all the time unless I'm in class or grading papers. So far it hasn't interrupted my sleep, but then that's very rarely an issue for me. You can ask Jesse's sister. In our college days, she used to say that my minor was sleep. I also have an excellent watchdog."

"Good to hear. I'm sure I don't need to tell you to call me if any of that changes."

"You don't."

"Are you still thinking of publishing a paper when the investigation is over?" she asked.

"Yes. In fact, I've already started some preliminary research and have been gathering sources to support my working theory. I honestly wasn't sure I'd still want to pursue the paper after leaving the investigation, but I can't let this kind of opportunity go. Besides, I really want to know what makes this jerk tick."

"I get that and I think it's a healthy way to cope with this unusually stressful situation. I hope I'll be able to read your paper."

I assured her that she would. We spent a few more minutes chatting, and then I left to go back to campus.

*****

I generally don't give much thought to the fact that I live alone; it suits me. I have plenty of friends and can be as social as I want, but I appreciate my solitude as well. My time away from work is my own, and if I want to stay up late reading or watching a movie, or if I decide to do yoga in the middle of the living room at 6:00 a.m., I'm not inconveniencing anyone. I can come and go as I please without having to consult anyone, except Cody, of course. I stick to a reasonably healthy diet, eating little prepackaged food, and have been a vegetarian for nearly thirty years. Even so, I can be incredibly lazy about feeding myself and go for a week or more without making what my mother would consider a proper meal. I suppose it's something you get used to, but I honestly don't know how people manage to cook actual dinners seven nights a week.

It's always great to have Cait stay with me. I genuinely enjoy her company as we hang out and talk, cook, and eat together. But I didn't take to moping around my "too quiet" house once she'd gone home, as one of my colleagues, a woman who "couldn't imagine living alone," suggested. Besides, she'd be back in town for Christmas, if not before. To each her own, I guess, and as I tell my pop culture students, wouldn't it be boring if we all liked the same things and behaved the same way? I spent the evening going over lecture notes for the following day's classes and reading student papers. I kept looking at the mystery novel on my coffee table. It was the latest from one of my favorite authors that I'd picked up the last time I was in the Bay Area. I have a strong opinion about buying books from real bookstores, preferably independents, and will bend the ear of anyone willing to listen to me about the importance of us all doing just that. Now, though, the thought of a murder mystery just didn't sit right. I was sure Mr. Crais would understand.

I let Cody out to do his business around ten thirty while I washed my face and brushed my teeth. When I opened the back door, I was surprised to see he wasn't waiting to come in, as he knows the routine we go through every single night. I called him, quietly enough so as not to bother the neighbors, but he didn't respond. I turned on the patio light, stepped outside, and spotted him in the far corner of the yard, staring at the fence. It took me a moment to realize I was hearing his low, menacing growl, which he very rarely does. If I had hackles, they'd be standing up as high as his. I slipped on the old sneakers I keep by the back door and walked toward him, continuing to call his name, and finally got his attention. He seemed torn for a few seconds, wanting to obey but unwilling to leave whatever it was on the other side of the fence that had him so freaked out.

I called again, and he finally came to me. I grabbed his collar and started walking him toward the house.

He stopped midstride and sniffed at a little clump of something I couldn't see well in the dark. I nudged it with my foot, and he went after it. I yanked his collar, told him to leave it, and finally got him inside. I shut and locked the door, my heart pounding. This is generally a very safe area, as Samantha had said the evening we discussed starting a neighborhood watch program. We rarely have to worry about cars or houses being broken into, and there's never been any violence or gang activity since I've lived here. Most people are good about keeping pets inside at night, as we have creatures that own the neighborhood after dark: roof rats, like the one I'd received at work, skunks, raccoons, and opossums. But I've never seen Cody react so fiercely to any of them.

I went into the living room, wanting to get away from the kitchen windows that have no blinds and set the alarm. I was hesitant to bother Jesse, as it was almost eleven o'clock, but I didn't think I'd be able to go to sleep as rattled as I was, and I certainly couldn't call 911 and say my dog was growling at the back fence. After a brief mental debate, I sent a text asking if he was awake. He called almost immediately after I'd tapped Send.

"Hey, sorry to bother you so late," I began.

"Don't worry about it. What's up?"

I quickly told him what happened, feeling a little ridiculous saying it out loud, but I was fairly sure Jesse didn't think I was given to hysteria.

"Cody doesn't growl like that at other animals, not even wild ones like opossums or raccoons."

"This is why you have a dog. I'm going to check in with the black and white in your area and then I'll be over."

"You don't have to come over—it's so late."

"But I'm going to. I won't be able to rest until I see with my own eyes that everything is okay. I may be off the case, but I'm still responsible for your safety, Ashley. I'll be there in twenty minutes or so."

"Okay. Thanks, Jesse. See you soon."

We disconnected and I concentrated on breathing and getting my heart rate back to normal.

I peeked out the front blinds when I heard a car engine idling. Jesse had arrived and was crouched down, talking to the passenger in the patrol unit. I watched until he stood up, tapped the roof with the palm of his hand, and turned toward my front door. He knocked once and said, "It's me."

Cody, who hadn't left my side since we came back into the house, gave a short warning bark as I deactivated the alarm and opened the door. I had a hold of his collar and pulled him back to give Jesse enough room to get inside and then shut and locked the door. He put his hand on my shoulder and asked, "You okay?"

"Yeah. Yeah, I'm fine," I said, more to myself than him. "Thanks for coming. I feel a little silly dragging you over here in the middle of the night."

"Would you stop that? You were right to call me. I told the guys in the black and white to be extra vigilant tonight, and they'll call me and Ed if they see anything weird. Are the people who live behind you home?"

"I don't know. They're pretty quiet, so I'm not sure I'd even notice if they weren't."

"Okay, I was just curious."

We sat on the couch, and Cody finally relaxed enough to wag his tail at Jesse, who patted his head and said, "Good job tonight, buddy."

I was starting to relax too. I'm not one to get jumpy over every odd noise or weird shadow, but a serial killer had demonstrated that he knew far too much about me. It was not a stretch to think he could discover my address.

"I don't suppose you'd consider calling in sick tomorrow," Jesse said.

I glanced at the clock on the mantle, seeing that it was eleven forty-five. I didn't anticipate getting more than a few hours of sleep, but I wasn't sure what calling in would accomplish.

"I guess I could," I said. "But what good would that do?"

He rubbed his eyes. "I don't know…maybe none. It just seems like it would be easier to make sure you're safe if I know you're here."

"What about talking to campus security again? I can ask for an escort to and from my car. They'll make sure I'm never in the parking garage alone, and they might even be willing to assign someone to the building until this is over."

"I might be okay with that."

"I'm not trying to be difficult here, Jesse, really. I just don't want to let this completely disrupt my life and that of my students."

"I don't need to remind you that we're dealing with a murderer, do I?"

"No, you don't. It's just that…if I give into fear and basically go into hiding…I don't know how I'll climb back out."

He considered that, but I could tell he wasn't happy. Unfortunately, the only thing that would truly ease his mind was the killer being caught and put away. And now that Jesse was off the case, he was going to have to watch from the sidelines and hope that Ed and Lisa Choe found a way to do that. I could only guess how frustrating that must be. But knowing Jesse, he would never even mention that. I wondered if he'd consider talking to Colleen.

He sighed. "All right, we can talk more about this in the morning."

"Okay. Thanks for coming over so late," I said, standing up.

"I'm not going anywhere," he said. "This couch looks perfectly comfortable."

I wouldn't have asked him to stay but was enormously relieved he'd decided to. I brought him a pillow and a blanket, said good night, and went into my room, where, despite what I'd told Dr. Pereira, it took quite a while to fall asleep. I couldn't help but wonder if our psycho was gearing up for another sick play. The length of time between murders had been growing shorter, and I was bracing myself to hear about another. Was he now planning his next move? Or was he changing his game once again? I'd been removed from the investigation for my own safety, and Jesse's captain had removed him for endangering me, but neither of us could just walk away and pretend the investigation wasn't always on our minds.

A few hours later, I awoke from a nightmare with a start, my heart pounding. The image faded as I fully woke up, but it took a few moments to shake the disturbing feeling. In the dream, I was desperately searching for my car in the parking garage at school, aware that someone—or something—was stalking me, getting closer at every turn. My desperation grew each time I turned down an aisle and didn't find my car. I needed to get the hell out of there, but in that awful way of nightmares, I was moving so slowly I may as well have been slogging through quicksand. I didn't need to reach for a Freud textbook to figure out what that one meant.

It was just after 5:00 a.m., but I knew there was no point in trying to go back to sleep. It was chilly in the house, so I put on some sweats and was about to open my bedroom door when I heard a noise in the living room and panicked. Cody was right beside me, so what *was* that? Oh, right—Jesse. He'd come to the rescue in response to my late-night text. I stood for a moment with my head against the door and my hand on the knob while I caught my breath. I was bringing jumpiness to new levels. As I passed the living room on the way to the kitchen to make coffee, I saw Jesse tying his shoes. The neatly folded blanket and pillow lay on the arm of the couch. Cody bounded over to greet our guest.

"Hey," Jesse said, scratching the dog's ears, "here's the superstar watchdog." Looking up at me, he asked, "How you doing?"

"I'm okay. Thanks again for coming over so late. Did you get any sleep?"

"I can sleep anywhere. How about you?"

"A few hours. Want some coffee?"

"Please," he said, getting up to follow me into the kitchen.

Cody went to the back door, and Jesse unlocked and opened it, watching the dog run outside. I glanced out the window and saw my watchdog protector go past the illumination cast by the back patio light, dashing for the far corner of the yard.

"That's where he was last night when he was growling and wouldn't come in."

I looked over in time to see Jesse sprint out the door. "What's wrong?" I asked, hurrying out after him. Jesse had Cody by the collar and was keeping him away from an opossum. I didn't realize the animal was dead until I was right next to it. Even in the dim predawn light, I could see its vivid red eyes and the blood and bile around its mouth. I looked at Jesse.

"Poison?"

He nodded. "Take Cody into the house."

Jesse's posture changed as he went into full-on cop mode. He activated the flashlight on his phone and probed the lopsided gray ball I'd seen the night before with a twig. It had little flecks of blue and red in it.

"What is that? Cody saw it last night after he finally came to me. I had to pull him away to keep him from going after it."

"You didn't touch it, did you?"

"Just with the toe of my shoe—"

"Throw those shoes away and get the dog into the house. Do it now, Ashley."

Hot tears stung my eyes as the realization hit. Raw hamburger meat. A dead opossum. In *my* yard. I ran to the side of the house, kicked my shoes off, and, holding them by the laces, tossed them into the trash can. Cody and I went inside, and my fear turned to rage. That son of a bitch tried to kill Cody. He came to my home intending to poison my dog. Jesse came inside a few minutes later and found me sitting on the floor with my arms around Cody, sobbing.

I'd calmed down considerably by the time I'd showered and gotten ready for work. I was still angry enough to punch something—or someone—but felt like I could function. As determined as I was to go about my day and act as though everything were normal, I didn't want to leave Cody at home alone for nine hours. Jesse was not at all happy about my reluctance to call in sick but grudgingly agreed that it wouldn't really accomplish anything. He offered to take Cody to the station and leave him in the capable hands of the K-9 supervisor. That seemed like the best option since I couldn't bring him to work with me. Cody happily leapt into Jesse's car, and the two of them followed me to campus, where Jesse spoke with the head of security while I went to class.

21

After a busy day at school, which included talking to students after class and a nonstop procession during office hours, I drove through the rain and arrived home to a warm house that smelled of homemade soup. Having a house guest had definite benefits. Cody met me at the door, and we went through our greeting routine and then into the kitchen to find Cait halfway through making a large green salad while a deliciously fragrant pot of soup simmered on the stove. She'd apparently paused to take a phone call and didn't look happy. She ended the call and looked up at me.

"Hey, everything okay?" I asked.

"I'm honestly not sure. I was just talking to Jesse. He's really having a tough time. Being removed from the investigation was not only a major blow to his ego, but he feels like he failed."

"I was afraid of that. I knew he wouldn't admit it, but it was all over his face the day he told me he was reassigned."

"That's not the worst of it. He won't stop beating himself up over getting you involved. Your being in danger is making him completely crazy. I don't think he's sleeping much."

"Dammit, that's not good. He most likely won't talk to me, but do you know if he's had a chance to see the department psychologist?"

"He didn't say, but knowing my brother, he thinks he needs to handle this on his own."

"This from the guy who insisted I talk to her. Nice double standard."

"You know how men are. They think asking for help is a sign of weakness."

I sighed. "True, but these are rather extraordinary circumstances."

"You don't need to tell me that. I'm probably just overreacting and going into big sister mode, but I'm worried about him."

"Yeah, me too, but I'm not sure what either of us can do. I wonder if he's talked to Ed. It seems like Jesse looks up to him."

"He does, for sure. Maybe I can talk him into that."

"Please try. Thanks for making dinner, it smells fantastic," I said. "Want to move in and be my personal chef?"

She smiled. "I have expanded my culinary repertoire since our dorm days."

"Um, yeah. Much less ramen."

Cait had taken care of everything for dinner, so after feeding the dog, I set the table, got us each a glass of water, opened a bottle of wine, and sat down. We went through the particulars of our days, and then Cait said she thought she was close to a breakthrough regarding Daniel and his situation, which didn't surprise me. Not only is Cait relentless at finding the facts she's after, but cooking is her version of a victory lap.

"So what did you find out?" I asked.

"I kept thinking how odd it was for Evan to call me that day. Like I said, we barely know each other, and I didn't even know he had my number. I realized that I really don't know anything about him. I never gave his background any thought because obviously Daniel thinks highly of him, but I turned up some interesting tidbits."

I took a sip of wine. "Oh yeah? Like what?"

"He's been audited twice and dodged a potential fraud case five years ago."

"Wow. That does not sound like a great business partner. Does Daniel know about any of this?"

"I don't know yet. I don't want to confront him until I see if any of it is relevant. He might be totally legit as far as the business is concerned. Maybe he just had a patch of bad luck at one point."

A possibility, but I could see she didn't buy it. Neither did I.

"So what are you going to do next?"

"Call Evan. I'd really like a face-to-face meeting, but I might have to settle for a phone call."

"Will he talk to you? Without getting suspicious, I mean."

"I think so. I can get him to believe I'm worried about Daniel, which is still true."

"Does Evan know that you haven't been able to reach Daniel?"

"No, at least not as far as I know."

I could tell she was working through something, so I didn't interrupt.

"Try this scenario," she began. "Say that Evan needs to get his hands on a lot of cash quickly, so he empties the company savings account and stashes the money somewhere Daniel couldn't get at it, even if he knew where it was."

I nodded. "Okay..."

"Then Evan calls me, telling me that Daniel is the one who closed the account and that he's going to go to the cops if he doesn't hear from him by the end of the week."

"Why would Evan bother to call you?"

"To have a witness who would say under oath that she was told the bank called Evan asking for verification that the account was to be closed. Since Daniel and I aren't married, I could be forced to testify against him."

"So why might Evan need cash?"

"Two things that come to mind immediately are drugs and gambling, but I don't think Evan has a drug problem. Daniel would most likely know about it if he did, so that leaves gambling. Daniel has mentioned that Evan goes to Vegas a lot. I just assumed he likes the vibe. Maybe he does—too much."

"If Evan is up to no good, he might be laying the groundwork to paint Daniel as the bad guy."

"Exactly."

I served us each some salad while Cait dished up the soup, another fabulous recipe she'd discovered in Morocco.

"This is incredible," I said. "Who knew I'd benefit so much from your going to Africa."

"Discovering new recipes is definitely one of the perks of traveling as much as I do. But I've also had to eat some things you don't want to know about."

"Please spare me," I said, holding up a hand. "You've already mentioned fried insects and snakes. I don't need to know any more than that."

"Don't worry, I know better than to upset my host."

We ate in contented silence for a few minutes.

"Speaking of Vegas," I said, "what's the latest on Casino Guy?"

"He's definitely involved with a Russian-run chop shop in West Sac, the one the Feds have been watching off Enterprise. They got a warrant to access his phone records, which allowed them to make the case for a tap."

"Wouldn't someone like him use a burner phone?"

"Sometimes, but you'd be surprised how many criminals don't. The arrogance of these guys—the serious ones who have several rackets going—would amaze you. They really think they're so good they'll never get caught."

Much like a serial killer, I thought. "So how does money laundering fit in? The chop shop certainly isn't generating legitimate income, so is he somehow running that money through his casino?"

"That's another piece of the puzzle I need to place, and I *will* figure it out."

She would. I thought about the things that drive different people. We all have our ways of getting a rush. For Cait, it was when that last puzzle piece falls into place and she can finally see the big picture. Mine was seeing the light go on in a student's eyes. And the killer... we were all too aware of how he was getting his rush and why he was reaching for more.

After we ate, I cleared the table and loaded the dishwasher, telling Cait to sit and have another glass of wine since she'd done the cooking. As I sometimes do during such moments, I wondered what it would have been like to grow up with a sister and if we'd be as close as Cait and I are. And I was once again thankful that we remain connected as life takes us in such different directions. I'd tearfully told Cait about the night Cody was nearly poisoned, prompting uncharacteristic tears of her own. Cait's made of tougher stuff than I am, and in all the years I've known her, I've rarely seen her cry, while she's dried my tears countless times. Since the incident, I'd been doing a thorough search of the yard before letting Cody out. After about a week, he stopped bolting for the fence but still seemed on high alert. The rain had stopped for the time being, and despite the cold and the soggy grass, we all went outside and tossed the ball for a bit, Cait marveling at Cody's endless energy.

22

H e woke up in a fog of confusion, unsure of where he was for a few moments. He'd angered the Other somehow. What had he done? He'd been incredibly careful with all his events, meticulously planning each detail, taking great care not to leave any evidence that could be traced to him at the scenes. He'd even been keeping an eye on the smarty-pants professor's house, but there hadn't been much activity other than a woman who seemed to stay there periodically and the black and white cruising the neighborhood. He'd always been in awe of the darkness, the power that the Other commanded, but they worked as one, so it was his power too.

Now, knowing that the Other was angry and realizing that power could be taken from him left him frustrated. That went against the agreement they'd made all those years ago. What would happen next? What would he do if the Other went away forever? There must be a way to make things right. He shuffled into the kitchen to make some tea and think things through. If he'd made a misstep somewhere along the way, perhaps he could atone for it somehow. Being careful and doing things in just the right way, that was how he kept order and made everything work—from his simple daily tasks to his special events. Boil the water, put the herbs in the infuser, and pour the water over the herbs. Order. Maintaining order pleased the Other.

He turned on the television and clicked through the channels. No one was talking about his last event, not even the cable news station. That was disappointing. Was that the problem? He wasn't commanding enough attention? Then a strange thought occurred. He might be able to keep the Other from leaving, but it would take a huge event, something he'd never dared think about before. He paced around his living room as the idea started to take shape. And as he put together his plan, he started to get angry. A deal was a deal, and it was supposed to last forever. Many years ago, he had promised the Other that he would never betray their confidence, never talk about their special plans. When that idiot school psychologist tried to get him to tell her about the "bad thoughts" and he'd refused, she told him if he didn't talk to her, she couldn't help him. The dumb cow couldn't help no matter what he told her. He had kept up his end of the bargain, and now the Other was going to leave? He couldn't let that happen. No, that wouldn't do. If the Other were going to go, they'd have to go together. It was time to get busy.

*****

Despite the calendar declaring it was still a week away, winter had come to the valley, bringing overnight low temperatures near freezing. The fog had vanished for the time being, leaving icy clear nights and daytime views of snow in the Sierra Mountains. The weather service issued frost warnings in the wine country and surrounding area farms and cautioned those of us in older homes to wrap exposed pipes to prevent freezing and bursting. The later sunrise starting in the fall had already ended my runs for the year, leaving me with the stationary bike instead, but I'm also too much of a wimp to run on a thirty-degree morning, much to Cody's dismay. His winter coat had come in, and he didn't seem to notice the drop in temperature. The semester was winding down, and students were gearing up for their last push to complete papers, research projects, and take final exams. That meant a major push for me as well with papers to read, exams to grade, and grant proposal deadlines to make.

I drove into the faculty parking garage and found a spot. I didn't see the security guard and honestly felt a little silly about calling and asking for someone to walk me to class. Then again, I was all too aware that the killer was someone who could move around the university freely and had obviously been doing so without attracting attention. Jesse and I had determined it unlikely that our suspect was a student, so who did that leave? A faculty member? Someone from maintenance, grounds keeping, or administration? I decided playing by Jesse's rules was the way to go and dialed the number. A few minutes later, my escort appeared, and we made the trek to Amador Hall without incident.

I spent most of the Psych 101 class reassuring my students they'd survive finals week. The first semester of college can be overwhelming, and those who choose to jump into a university right out of high school without the benefit of a stopover at a community college can convince themselves they aren't going to make it. Trying to get them to focus on what they'd accomplished, I steered the discussion toward the goal setting we'd talked about the first day of class. And as my brain likes to do at the most inopportune times, it reminded me that Jesse had called and left his first message during that very class. Four months had gone by quickly. I'd seen the atrocities a deeply troubled mind can create, and my worldview had shifted. While it was true I'd been given a unique vantage point from which to observe psychopathic behavior, that access had come with a price. I was now a different person.

Once I'd become involved with the investigation, I stopped listening to the news and reading it online. I didn't want the media to color my opinion of the facts Jesse was sharing with me, but I also just wanted a break. I had suspected that the deeper I went, the more the case would take hold of me, and I was right. Avoiding the news was my attempt to set boundaries and retain a sense of normalcy, and I hadn't gone back to it after leaving the investigation. It felt kind of nice to be blissfully unaware of what was going on beyond the confines of the university and my little world. As a result, I missed a local story that was running parallel to what Cait was investigating. After my Psych 101 class, Angelica came into our office with that day's newspaper. A traditionalist, Ang still prefers to get her news in print.

"Have you been following this story about the luxury car thefts happening around town?"

"No, I haven't really been paying much attention to the news lately," I said, barely looking away from the test I was grading. She dropped the paper on my desk, partially covering the test.

"Car theft is much more common than we'd like to think, unfortunately, but this is different. There's been a string of high-end thefts over the past few months. These cars are coming into Sacramento, but they're disappearing from the port and never making it to the dealerships."

That got my attention. I looked at the article, scanning for any mention of Vegas or Romano, the man Cait was investigating and referred to as Casino Guy.

"Actually, I did hear about this. Cait's been working on a story involving a casino owner in Vegas who's suspected of a number of things, including being involved with a car theft ring."

"Really? Does she think he has anything to do with the thefts at the port?"

"It looks like it at this point."

"Wow, so this might be a dual-state operation. Anyway, the whole thing is fascinating. Take a look at this article when you have a minute, and you should read the earlier articles online when you can."

I'd do that as soon as I had time. Cait hadn't said much about her ongoing investigation lately, and I understood her reluctance to discuss her findings until she knew what she was dealing with, but she was spending quite a lot of time in Vegas, getting more entrenched, and was now completely convinced that Evan was working to set up Daniel. Was Evan dangerous? Maybe. Was Casino Guy? Definitely. But after our heated discussion last month, I was trying to keep from telling her how worried I was about her safety. She was methodically working her way through the facts, gathering more information, and I just had to have faith that she'd figure out what was going on while being able to keep herself out of harm's way.

I brought a cup of soup and a salad from the cafeteria back to my desk and looked up the newspaper archives, searching for any stories having to do with stolen high-end cars, the luxury dealerships in town, and the port. I found three and read them in chronological order. As Angelica had mentioned, the first article explained that expensive cars bound for the high-end dealerships in town were coming into Sacramento via the port but never making it out, corroborating what Cait had discovered. The owner of Von Housen, the capital city's Mercedes dealer for more than fifty years, gave a brief interview, saying he'd never experienced anything like this, losing ten cars in the past four months. The cars he'd purchased were on a ship, arrived at the port, and then never made it onto the truck. He went on to explain that whoever was behind the thefts was obviously being careful in that he never lost an entire shipment—it was always a car or two here and there with no discernable pattern. He said it had taken a while for him to realize what was going on.

The next article focused on a customer who had special-ordered a Jaguar he never got to drive and interviews with members of various car clubs in town, and the third laid out the theory that it had been so far impossible to locate the chop shop because it was mobile. The crew packed up their minimal equipment every few days and moved to a new location, staying a step or two ahead of the police, who needed a new warrant each time they wanted to search a different building. Interesting theory. I had no idea what sort of equipment or how much was needed to strip a car, but with a large enough crew who knew what they were doing, maybe not that much. They could possibly pack everything they needed into a truck and unpack when they found their next location. I spent the rest of the afternoon before my last class reviewing student research projects and fine-tuning lecture notes for that class.

Cait had gone back to The City to try to meet with Evan. She planned to come back for the weekend, but that might change. I was completely out of sorts that evening, and it had nothing to do with my intermittent house guest. I'd finished reading student papers while still on campus and had gone over my lecture notes for the next day. It was the kind of cold, dreary night that was perfect for curling up with a mug of hot chocolate and a book or watching a movie, neither of which I had the attention span to do. I was restless. I'd tried to mentally distance myself from the investigation after leaving, and when Jesse was reassigned, I was another layer away. I should have gone on ignoring the news and focused on the coming end of the semester and finals week and getting ready for Christmas. But all I could think about was when—not if—the killer was going to strike again and how I'd failed to provide Jesse with any useful information. Oh, and said killer obviously knew where I live. Happy freakin' holidays.

Okay, enough was enough. Aimlessly wandering around my house because I couldn't figure out what to do with myself was getting me nowhere and was extremely annoying. I have little tolerance for my own whininess, so I decided that going into research mode would snap me out of my funk. I grabbed my laptop and the file full of notes I'd been compiling for the research paper I planned to publish once the investigation was over. I settled on the couch and got to work. Jesse, Ed, and I had sketched a bare-bones profile of the killer based on the reports made at the scenes of the crimes. But what I hadn't yet done was provide an in-depth analysis of the specific type of psychosis I thought we might be dealing with.

Psychopathy presents in different ways within individuals, but common traits include lack of empathy, overconfidence or even narcissism, and a low tolerance for frustration, which can often lead to violence. And while multiple personality disorder, or dissociative identity disorder, as it's now more commonly called, is still a controversial diagnosis, I wasn't ruling that possibility out. I'd also have to look at borderline personality disorder and good old classic schizophrenia. Publishing a paper would certainly be satisfying, and doing this research along the way might help provide some insight that could lead to catching the killer. It just felt completely wrong that Jesse wouldn't be the one that insight would help. Browsing, reading articles, and adding to my growing pile of notes calmed my restlessness, and I was able to maintain my detachment and stay in clinical mode. Most people wouldn't be comfortable with researching psychopathy and related disorders before bed, but I guess I'm not most people. I had no trouble sleeping that night.

23

The next morning, I turned into the university from J Street and immediately came to a stop in a huge line of cars. Campus security was out in force, attempting to direct traffic. I could see the flashing lights of emergency vehicles in the distance, and it looked like State University Drive was blocked off farther down. Wondering what could have happened that would create so much commotion, I inched my way forward along with everyone else and finally made the turn onto Arboretum to get to the faculty parking garage. It seemed pointless to call security for my escort, as there were so many people in the garage, plus I doubted anyone was available at the moment. Walking along with the crowd, I heard snippets of conversation and speculation as to what was going on. Had there been an accident? Maybe someone had a heart attack. Then a woman said, "I heard they found a body in the river by the Guy West Bridge." Heart pounding, I pulled my phone out of my bag, nearly dropping it, and called Jesse. It went straight to voice mail. Dammit! I hurried into my building and ran up the stairs.

The department chair was coming down the hallway as I approached my office, apparently making the rounds. She told everyone within earshot that unless we were otherwise told, classes were to go ahead as scheduled. There had been no official statement as to why there were emergency vehicles on campus, but she would notify us as information became available. I sat down at my desk as Angelica walked in.

"Do you know what's going on? Have you talked to your cop? People are saying they found a body in the river."

Yet again, proof that horrible news—if that's what really happened—travels fast.

"No, I don't know, and I was just about to try Jesse again." I got his voice mail once more and left a short message to please call as soon as he could. I had an hour before my first class and should have used the time to read student papers but instead went online to see if the major news stations had any mention of what was going on at the university on their websites. I found nothing of substance. One station was running a video shot from their helicopter, showing an aerial view of the campus and the activity around the bridge, but they had "no further information to report at this time." Angelica thought that meant that whatever had happened must not be terribly newsworthy. I wanted her to be right but knew she wasn't. The killer had struck again, and the cops were doing their best to keep the media as quiet as possible.

Jesse sent a text right before I had to go to class. He was in a meeting but would call as soon as he was able. The fact that he didn't tell me the incident on campus had nothing to do with our psycho convinced me that it did. I gathered my lecture notes, and Angelica and I headed for the pop culture class. I knew that as much as I enjoy it, I'd have a nearly impossible time concentrating. My students weren't any more able to focus since most of them had already heard the rumor about a body in the river. I put my notes aside and began talking about why horrific events get sensationalized and what that does to our ability to process information. Ang brought up how being exposed to the relentless 24-7 news cycle, which focuses on the negative and is certainly driven by social media, may affect the way we interpret and interact with the world around us.

I could see that not everyone was fully on board with that idea, so I thought of a way to illustrate the point.

"So by now, it seems that everyone has heard the rumor about the body in the river, right?"

Nods and murmurs of agreement.

"If none of you had smart phones or social media accounts, or let's say you couldn't even go into the library and get online, how would you go about finding out what happened here today?"

My students considered that for a bit, and then one said he'd listen to the radio on his way home. Another said she'd watch the evening news.

"Okay, and that would be, what, seven or eight hours from now?" They agreed. "Now, take out your phones—and this is the only time I'll ever ask you to do so in one of my classes—and look for a reference to the story. It can be anything from a brief comment to video footage from the news van that's been parked by the bridge."

They all did as asked, and I watched their faces. "Did anyone not find at least a mention?" No one.

"It's on the homepage of the local paper's website," said Kellye.

Marc said, "It's the trending topic on all of the social media sites I use."

"I found a video, a still pic with a headline, and got a breaking news alert," said Debbie.

"And all of that was instantly accessible the minute you looked for it. If you go about your normal day going online, interacting on social media, and just walking around campus, how many more times do you think you'll hear about the body found in the river?"

"A bunch" seemed to be the consensus.

"And each time you hear about it, do you think you'll become more upset or less so? Will you keep thinking about the poor person who lost their life right out there"—I pointed in the general direction of the bridge—"or will this story just become one of the many depressing, traumatic events we're bombarded with every day and fade into the background noise?"

They decided that it would likely be the latter without a concerted effort. Then Lori asked, "So what can we do about that?"

We spent the rest of the class discussing ways to step back from the relentless negativity without becoming isolated and uninformed.

Jesse had called during class and left a message asking if I could meet him for lunch at a nearby café. The minute I saw him, I knew why he'd wanted to meet in person. I could see it in his eyes—something big had happened. He greeted me with a smile, and we stood in line to order.

"So you obviously saw all the commotion on campus this morning."

"I did. And?"

He lowered his voice. "A cyclist crossing the bridge around seven fifteen this morning saw something ominous-looking in the river, went to investigate, and saw that it was in fact a body. He called it in, and Ed and Lisa were first on the scene."

"Was the body just…in the river? I mean, there wasn't any kind of scene staged?"

"Not like what we've been finding. The victim was a White male, likely in his forties, and the cause of death was listed as drowning, pending lab results. He had rosary beads wrapped around his hands and a small Bible and a suicide note in a plastic bag in his jacket pocket."

It took a moment for me to absorb the last thing Jesse said. "Wait. A suicide note?"

"Asking for forgiveness."

We'd reached the cashier by then. I had no idea what I wanted, so I impulsively chose a salad to go with the soup du jour. Jesse stopped me as I reached for my wallet, saying lunch was on him. He ordered and paid, and we found a table.

"Jesse, are you telling me that you think our guy killed himself?"

"That's what it looks like. What do you think? Would a psychopath do that?"

"They generally don't. Narcissism is a large element of that personality type, and people who think so highly of themselves rarely take their own lives. I suppose he might consider it if he were to get caught. The idea of going to prison for life could possibly make him take his own way out. But remember, our guy doesn't think he'll ever get caught—he's too clever. And asking for forgiveness just doesn't fit. He can't tell right from wrong, so his behavior is totally justified in his mind."

"Didn't you say psychopaths are good at pretending to have normal emotions and telling people what they want to hear?"

"Yes, they are. I suppose this could be his way of handing us what we're supposed to believe is a neat little ending."

"But you don't believe it?"

"I don't know. Was there anything else on or around the body?"

"Not that they've found. The dive team is still checking it out."

"How long does it usually take to identify a victim?"

"This will be expedited. We should have an ID by this afternoon."

We sat in silence looking at each other for a moment, and then he smiled.

"So if this does actually turn out to be our lunatic…," I began.

"Then you're safe, Ashley. The nightmare is over, and you can have your life back."

I closed my eyes, wanting it to be true with every cell in my body.

"What's your gut feeling, Jesse? Is it really him? Did he tire of his game and decide to end it for good?"

"My gut says yes. This is finally over. How about you?"

I hesitated. "Well, I'm still stumbling over the note. In his mind, there's nothing to forgive him for—in fact, he has no sense of forgiveness because he has no concept of remorse. And as much as I want this to be over, like I said, psychopaths very rarely kill themselves." Then something occurred to me. "But on the other hand, I suppose it might be possible that he had a complete break with the element of his personality that was driving him to kill."

The waitress brought our food. The café is known for locally sourced farm-fresh ingredients, and my farmhouse salad and tomato soup were fabulous. Jesse dug into his chicken sandwich. We ate in silence for a moment, and then he asked, "So does that mean he has—or had—multiple personalities? Like, different voices in his head?"

"Maybe. Unfortunately, none of this is black and white, and multiple personality, or what we now call dissociative identity disorder, is a controversial diagnosis because there isn't a clear consensus on the criteria or treatment. And of course, psychosis presents a little differently in each individual. But if he did have that break, he would need to get away from that personality element, essentially quiet that voice, and it could be that taking his own life was the only way he saw to do that."

"You still don't seem convinced," Jesse said.

"I'm not 100 percent convinced. Not yet. Probably because my wanting this to be true so badly is making me hold out for irrefutable proof."

"Well then, I'm going to do my best to bring that to you."

It was good to see Jesse act like himself again. The sense of utter defeat I saw the day he told me he was off the case was gone, and in its place was that drive to be one of the good guys that's such a huge part of him. We finished our meals, and I thanked him for lunch.

"It's the least I can do," he said, "until I bring you that proof."

We walked outside into the weak December sunshine, said goodbye, and then headed in opposite directions.

I got back to campus to discover that classes had been cancelled for the remainder of the day. Detective Marquez appeared briefly on the noon news, saying that a body had been found in the river near the bicycle bridge and that it appeared to be an accidental drowning. He didn't stay long enough to take questions from reporters. The dean made an announcement relaying that information, made sure the counseling center was fully staffed, and cancelled classes. Angelica and I walked out to the parking garage, and it dawned on me that if it was in fact the killer who had been found in the river that morning, I wouldn't have to call for security to walk out to my car anymore. That sure felt good. It was starting to sink in that the nightmare might really be over. I said goodbye to Ang, got in my car, and sent Cait a quick text telling her I had possible good news to share and that dinner was on me when she got back into town tomorrow.

24

The hostess was showing Cait and me to our table when I heard a familiar voice say, "Hey, Ashley!"

Oh great, Lester again. I sincerely hoped he wouldn't start showing up as much as he had in my Tower days. He followed us to our table, and I quickly introduced Cait, saying we had a lot to catch up on and hoping he'd get the message and leave us alone. Nope, not Lester.

"Lester works for the classic rock station in town," I told Cait.

"Not anymore," he said. "I'm over at the news station now."

"Oh, good for you, congrats."

"Thanks. It was a good move. I'm still in sales, of course, but I've always wanted to get involved with the news. You just might hear me on the air one of these days."

I gave him a half-hearted thumbs-up and said we were going to look at the menus. He finally took the hint and went back to his table.

"I take it he's not one of your favorite people," Cait said.

"It's that obvious? Yeah, Lester is…exhausting. I first met him when I was at Tower. He was new to radio sales back then and was constantly after me to buy into every promotion he could think of. It got worse once I went to the advertising department. Then he never left me alone."

"That does sound pretty annoying."

"One of the blank tape reps used to refer to him as an ankle biter."

She looked confused. "Huh?"

"You know, like one of those yappy little dogs that nips at your ankles."

She laughed. "Wow. You guys really didn't like him."

"Yeah, not so much."

The waitress came by to tell us the specials, took our orders, and hurried off.

"So you said you had good news?" Cait said.

"Did you hear about the drowning at the college yesterday?"

"I did, but how could that possibly be good news?"

I leaned forward and quietly said, "They think it's the killer."

"Really? Are they sure?"

"Not yet, but it's looking pretty good."

I went through the conversation I'd had with Jesse and why it could be that the body in the river was in fact our psycho. I also briefly went through my reservations as to why I thought it might not be.

"But if it is, that means you're safe—you can have your life back."

"Yes. And Jesse can get on with his job and not have this horrible thing hanging over his head."

She smiled. "That's fantastic. I'll call him after dinner."

The waitress brought our food, and we spent a few minutes in silence, enjoying the meal. I was curious about the latest with Daniel and didn't have to wait long for her to mention him.

"I saw Daniel Wednesday night."

"You did? When did he get back?"

"Early Tuesday morning. He texted me when he finally got out of that little village and back to Freiburg. Luckily, he didn't have to hang around the airport too long and was able to get a flight out within a few hours."

"I'm sure he was glad to be home," I said.

"Yeah, he was until he went into the office and found two FBI agents waiting for him."

"At his office? How did they know he'd be there, and what did they want?"

"The Feds can find out where just about anyone is, and Daniel wasn't trying to hide, so they knew when and where he'd used his passport. They also knew when he landed at SFO."

Not a surprise, but that fact still gave me pause. There's really no such thing as anonymity in the modern world.

Cait continued. "They asked him about the bank account, which, of course, he knew nothing about since he'd been out of the country. It was his word against Evan's until the bank told the agents they had both signatures authorizing closing the account. They also wanted to know why he'd been in Germany, obviously—"

"Wait, back up a bit. The bank says they have both Daniel's and Evan's signatures?"

"That's right."

"So Evan forged Daniel's signature?"

"That's what it looks like."

"Can he prove that?"

"I don't know. I hope so…he's working on it. Obviously, Evan is claiming Daniel forged his."

"Did they hassle him about Germany?"

She smiled. "Not after he showed them some pictures he took of the Porsches."

"I bet that was effective. Guys and cars…"

"Right?"

Cait also brought me up to speed on the latest with Evan, telling me that she'd not only failed to get her face-to-face meeting with him but had also seen him in Vegas when he was supposed to be in Seattle, according to the office manager.

"You sure it was him?"

"I wasn't at first, so I followed him to a casino owned by…take a guess."

"Casino Guy?"

"Yep."

"Okay, a coincidence maybe, but that doesn't necessarily mean he's up to no good. Even if the office manager told you he was in Seattle, maybe he diverted to Vegas on the way home to have a few drinks and hit the slot machines."

"More like blackjack. I chatted up one of the dealers, told him I was doing a piece on high rollers, and asked if I could get his point of view. He wouldn't talk to me while he was on the clock, but I met him at a bar later that night, and he spilled his guts. Evan is in debt up to his eyeballs at that casino."

"How much is that? Like, twenty grand? Fifty?"

"More like $250,000."

"Holy crap! He's on the hook for a quarter million with this guy?"

"Yeah, which is why it's so likely that after he emptied the Your Dream Ride account and still owed Casino Guy $175,000, he got desperate. Maybe he's trying to work off that debt."

"Work it off how—oh geez, he's an accountant, so he'd know how to cook the books in all sorts of ways, wouldn't he?"

She nodded. "The cops think Casino Guy is guilty of money laundering, among other things."

"Do you think Evan would take that big a risk?"

"Yeah, I do. And I also think he'd try to pin it on Daniel."

She let out a heavy sigh, and I realized how much stress she'd been carrying since she had first spoken to Evan.

"But it's obvious that Daniel is cooperating with the Feds, so he's going to be fine. Right?"

She shook her head. "I honestly don't know."

We'd both lost our appetites by then and declined to-go boxes for the remainder of our meals. When we got back to my house, I suggested watching a silly sitcom to take our minds off things, but Cait just wanted to go to bed. I stayed up late staring at the TV with the dog but couldn't tell you what I watched.

The final few weeks of the semester are as busy for faculty as they are for the students. We have exams to grade and papers to read, and all grades must be submitted by the deadline. Students feel overwhelmed, and instructors often do as well, whether we admit it or not. As busy as I was, I spent less time thinking about the investigation and the possibility that it really had come to an end when the body was discovered by the Guy West Bridge that day. Cait flew to New York to cover a lightweight story about department store elves with plans to be back in the valley for Christmas. Not her typical kind of gig, but she said it was the perfect way to detox from the ongoing Vegas saga, and I once again marveled at her willingness to hop on a plane with a day's notice. My students managed to make it through finals week, and I managed to read all their papers, grade their exams, sign off grad student projects, and get grades submitted on time. Fall semester came to an end the week before Christmas, and I was more than ready for the five-week winter break.

25

I was sitting at the kitchen table, lingering over coffee, and skimming the news on my tablet the first day of break when Jesse sent a text. He'd been tasked with typing up the final reports for each murder book and the closing report for the investigation. When he got to the file on the man found in the river, he saw the suicide note for the first time, snapped a quick photo, and sent it to me, the text saying he thought I'd find it interesting. It would undoubtedly be more interesting than what I was reading in local news. I enlarged the picture enough to read the note. The author did indeed ask for forgiveness for "past transgressions," as Jesse had told me earlier, but he also wrote of a recent loss, calling it a catastrophic event but a necessary evil. How's that for an interesting word choice?

The note went on, the author declaring that the loss dictated only one potential outcome. I thought about that for a few minutes. It was possible that we—Jesse, Ed, Lisa, and I—were all being played. But it was also possible that the killer had in fact suffered a break with the part of his psyche that made him commit atrocities. And the only way to truly get away from that element would be to kill himself, and thus the element. As a rule, psychopaths don't feel what we think of as normal emotions, so the killer wouldn't fear death. They also tend to have a low threshold for frustration, which is what can lead to violent behavior. If the break with the homicidal element of his personality disrupted what he felt was his "normal" way of being, that could certainly cause frustration and maybe a sense of betrayal, although I don't think the concept of loyalty means anything to anyone with psychopathy.

One other possibility was that our guy had suffered a complete break with all the elements of his personality, and death was the only way to "quiet the voices," as Jesse had put it. I replied to his text, saying that I agreed the man found in the river was in fact our killer and thanked him for the proof he promised. We could all breathe easier now. It also occurred to me that the rosary, the Bible, and the sense of loss mentioned in the note might have been the killer's final puzzle. I thought that REM's "Losing My Religion" fit but decided not to text that to Jesse. The game was over, and we were done with creepy riddles.

I don't get too carried away with Christmas decorations, but I do insist on having a real tree, as the smell is an instant reminder of my childhood in the mountains. I also put up outdoor lights as nearly everyone in East Sac does. The sight of all the houses alight as I come into my neighborhood at night is incredibly cheerful. I hosted an informal Christmas party on the twenty-third, inviting Angelica, Tony, and a few others from the university, Stephen and Jason from Evolution Theory, Ian and Jeff from the club, and my neighbors from next door and across the street. Cody and I spent Christmas Day with my parents in Foresthill and were treated to deer sightings and a light dusting of snow. Cait breezed back into town to spend the holiday with her parents and Jesse and then was gone again a few days later, which was a bummer because she wouldn't be around for Evolution Theory's New Year's Eve show.

Jesse and I met for coffee one morning the week after Christmas at the café a few blocks from my house, where I'd first heard about the case. It felt as if that day were a lifetime ago. It was warm enough to sit outside, thanks to the sunshine, so I decided to bring the dog. We said our hellos and sat at a table with the sun warming our backs. Cody was overjoyed to see Jesse again, who scratched his four-legged admirer's ears and gave me the update on the official closing of the case.

"Ed and Lisa called it closed, and the captain agreed."

"So the guy in the river that day was definitely the killer?"

"Yes."

I let that sink in for a moment. "Who was he?"

"I can't give you his name, but I can tell you that he worked for the phone company for twenty-five years. He was apparently one of those guys who kept to himself. No one really knew him very well, and of course, no one knew he was completely nuts and capable of such violence."

I thought about the sequence of events and how the murders began to happen closer together around the same time that the clues started to point to the next crime. And then after the man was discovered in the river near campus, nothing else had happened. It really was over.

"Pardon me for going into clinical mode here, but this is really fascinating. As I told you before, it's highly unusual for psychopaths to take their own lives, but this would indicate that he suffered a total break from the part of his psyche that made him commit those horrible crimes. This is one for the books for sure."

"Are you still going to publish a research paper?"

"Yes. One of the things I'll do on this break is finish writing it. Now that this whole ordeal is over, I feel like I can finally do that."

Jesse was toying with his cup, staring at the table. "Uh, Ash..."

"What's wrong?" I asked.

"I don't think I ever properly apologized for dragging you into this."

"What? Come on, Jesse, we've been over this. I agreed to get involved. It's not like you strong-armed me into it."

"I know but I still seriously endangered you because I thought you could help me crack my first big case. You had a psycho walking around on campus, sending you nasty gifts, and staking out your house. He tried to poison your dog for god's sake." Jesse reached down to pat Cody.

"All true, but you had no way of knowing what would happen, and everything turned out okay. You don't owe me an apology."

"Okay, but I'm sorry, anyway."

"Accepted. Can we be done with that now?"

He nodded and gave me the thirteen-year-old smile, which I couldn't help but return. We left the case behind and chatted about Cait for a bit. I wasn't sure how much she'd told Jesse about Daniel,

Evan, and her investigation of Casino Guy. He was mostly up to speed, but I noticed a few pertinent details missing, like Casino Guy's possible mob ties and Evan's early efforts to pin the missing company funds on Daniel. I wasn't surprised that Jesse had an abbreviated version of the investigation, and it certainly wasn't my place to tell her brother what Cait was dealing with. That was up to her, and I'd keep my mouth shut. I occasionally have the wisdom to do that.

"Hey," I said, "if you don't already have plans for Saturday night, you should come to Harlow's. My friend's band is part of their New Year's Eve show."

"The band you took Cait to see, Evolution something? She really liked them. Okay, yeah, that sounds good."

"Great. They're called Evolution Theory, and I think you'll like them too."

The sun had disappeared behind clouds by then, and it was getting a little chilly to sit outside. I told Jesse when the show would start and that he could get tickets on the venue's website, and then we said goodbye. I watched him walk to his truck, glad he was no longer shouldering the burden of being responsible for my safety but wondering how being forced to the sidelines while he watched his partner finish the investigation was affecting him. Experiencing a traumatic event with someone really does create an emotional bond; I needed to know that Jesse was going to be okay. Cody and I walked home down quiet streets past bare trees silhouetted against the slate-colored sky. I looked at the layers of gray and thought about another year coming to an end in the valley.

26

Spring semester had begun in late January and was off to a good start. I was teaching three classes, including Clinical Psychology, which I'd swapped with Angelica for Psych 101. The department chair likes to have us trade off so no one gets burned out on the intro course. The pop culture class was still only offered in the fall, and I was still hoping to change that eventually. Contemporary Issues in Psychology and The Psychology of Personality rounded out my course list. Committee and department meetings took a chunk of my schedule, and trading the intro course for a more advanced class meant more prep and grading time.

I'd finished my research paper, done a lot of pleasure reading, and completed a few projects around the house during the break between semesters. Cody and I had enjoyed that long break, and we were now getting back into our regular routine. He always takes a few days to adjust, following me around the house as I get ready in the morning, as if he's thinking, *Not this again…* And like any other devoted pet parent, I explain to him what's going on and my reason for being gone all day again. Someone will have to prove to me that he doesn't understand what I'm saying before I'll stop doing that.

Thursday afternoon, I was in my office going over lecture notes for my next class when Cait texted and said she'd be in town that weekend, chasing a lead. I wasn't sure if it was something new, or if she was still pursuing Daniel's ongoing issues with his partner that had begun last fall, as she hadn't given me any updates lately and I hadn't seen anything else about the car thefts in the news. I was especially looking forward to her visit this time. It's always great to see her, but I tend to get the blues in January. After all the holiday lights and decorations come down and the fog settles in to stay, it can be a bit bleak in the valley. It would be nice to have company to brighten things up. And no one brightens a room like Cait.

I stopped at a grocery store on my way home that night to pick up a few essentials and look for inspiration to make something special for dinner on Saturday since Cait had wowed me with her new recipes the last few times she was in town. I was walking down an aisle when I was intercepted by Lester.

"Hey, Ashley! I've been looking for you."

"Well, you found me. What's going on?"

"Is your reporter friend still in town?"

Wondering why he'd want to know if Cait were here, I said, "She's in The City today but will be back sometime this weekend. Why?"

"I was at the station today and heard the newscasters talking about all the hubbub over that car theft ring. They said your friend is doing some big investigative piece—her name's Caitlyn Malone, right?"

"Yeah, that's her—"

"So I can help her out!"

What? I stared at him. "Um, Les, she's been doing this for a long time. She knows how to find sources and track down leads."

"Yeah, I know. She's won awards and all that."

Cait would be so pleased to know that her Pulitzer was regarded as "awards and all that."

"But I bet she doesn't know about the warehouse in West Sac, does she?"

"What warehouse?" I asked.

He leaned forward as if he were about to reveal some top-secret info. "It just so happens that I know about a shipment of luxury cars that came in through the port but didn't make it to the dealership. The cops think they're hidden in a warehouse somewhere off Enterprise."

"So?"

"So she needs to check it out. Come on, Ashley, keep up!"

"Uh, sure, Les, I'll tell her," I said, intending to do no such thing. I started walking toward the checkout stand, and he turned and followed.

"Have her call me!"

"Yeah, I'll do that." Which would be difficult since I don't have his number. Ankle biter.

Cait arrived Saturday afternoon, looking radiant as always. How she manages to look so great with her crazy schedule never ceases to amaze me. It was a gray, chilly day and it had been raining intermittently, so I lit a fire and made hot cocoa. We sat on the couch with Cody between us and chatted about the new semester, my classes, and the latest on the Vegas story and Casino Guy.

"The tide has definitely turned," she said.

"How so?"

"The feds are all over Evan, and Daniel is fully cooperating, but the only thing he has in his favor at this point is proof that Evan forged his signature."

"He was able to prove that? How?"

"Handwriting analysis. Everyone has a uniquely individual signature, and even if someone practices and produces an excellent copy, the experts can tell. But Daniel doesn't have enough evidence to prove Evan guilty of anything else. Yet."

She went on to explain that if Evan emptied the company's savings account to pay down his Vegas debt, he likely paid Casino Guy in cash, so it would be nearly impossible to trace.

"Also, we don't have concrete evidence yet, but Evan is almost definitely the one doing the money laundering."

"You really think he'd take that chance?"

"If he was desperate enough. That would be a way to pay off a huge gambling debt."

"Wow. So Evan takes Casino Guy's dirty money from the car thefts and, what, runs it through a legit business somehow?"

"Pretty much," she said. "Money laundering has three basic steps—placement, where the dirty money is put into legitimate accounts, in this case Your Dream Ride's operational account. Layering, where the money is moved between accounts to make it hard to follow if someone takes interest is next. Then the final step is funneling the money back into Casino Guy's accounts so he can spend seemingly clean money."

It struck me then why Cait looked so radiant. She was about to put everything together and be able to tell her story at last. She was getting her rush, and the fact that she was also going to be instrumental in clearing Daniel no doubt helped.

By then, we'd swapped the cocoa for wine, and while I made dinner, she sat at the kitchen table and told me how she'd caught Evan lying.

"I'd been calling Evan's cell, trying to pin him down on a date to meet with me, and after a few lame excuses, he stopped answering. So I called the office and caught Helen, their admin, in a chatty mood. She told me Evan decided not to go to Germany with Daniel because it was so last minute and he didn't think they should both be out of country."

"Interesting," I said.

"Right? That was lie number one. Then Helen told me Evan was going to be in Seattle the following week, which I didn't give a second thought until I saw him in Vegas."

"He not only didn't want anyone to know he was in Vegas, he also needed Helen to say he was in Seattle if anyone asked about him."

She nodded. "Yep. Evan has been weaving quite the web of deceit, including laundering money for Casino Guy and, for all we know, helping feed cars into the chop shops. Now we just need enough evidence to prove it. And if we can..."

"Evan goes down for money laundering and grand theft auto."

"Yep. A neat little ending to a nasty saga, wouldn't you say?"

"Absolutely. And you and Daniel are going to make sure it ends that way."

"You can bet on it." She raised her wineglass with a smile.

As little as I know, or care to know, about the business world, I'm still fascinated by how many ways there seem to be to bend rules, get around regulations, and cheat people. And just blatantly break the law. I had to wonder if those inclined to do the cheating and stealing greatly outnumbered those who are not fundamentally changed or corrupted by making a lot of money. The answer, of course, is that they don't. We just don't hear about the good guys; they make for boring headlines.

Cait spent Sunday and most of Monday at her parents' house. Her mom was feeling a lot better but still needed to take it easy on her ankle. So Cait cleaned, took her shopping, and did some extra cooking, illustrating yet again the benefits of the freedom her job afforded. I devoted my Sunday to the menial domestic chores like laundry and cleaning the house, which aren't at all interesting but make you feel good when they're done. And with the right soundtrack: classic Journey, Cheap Trick, and Evolution Theory in this case, such chores are easily accomplished. Monday passed without incident. The Freshman Outreach Committee the department chair had drafted me for didn't appear as though it would take up all that much of my time, and I was hoping it might even be productive.

That night, I walked in the front door and was greeted by Cody. He then bounded over to Cait, who was sitting on the couch in the middle of a phone call. We waved hello, and I gestured for Cody to follow me into the kitchen where I put the groceries for the stir-fry I intended to make on the counter. Cait joined us a few minutes later when she'd wrapped up her call. We chatted about our days and what I planned to put into the stir-fry. Then I asked if she had any updates on the situation with Daniel and Evan.

"Maybe. Can we talk about that over dinner? I have another phone call to make and I have to look up something online."

"Sure. This won't take long to put together. We should be able to eat in about a half hour."

"Perfect and thank you for making dinner tonight."

"My pleasure. I owe you at least a few more."

Cait thought she was close to wrapping up her piece on Casino Guy, which had grown quite a bit more complicated once she discovered that Evan was involved. She brought me up to speed over dinner.

"The Sacramento cops got a big break when they picked up a guy from one of the chop shops. Apparently, he was supposed to do final cleanup on an abandoned site, and they caught him there by himself. He was here without a work visa and scared of being sent back to Russia. He played silent tough guy for a bit and then came clean to an interpreter."

That made sense. There's a large Russian population in West Sacramento. "So that adds hiring undocumented workers to Casino Guy's charges?" I asked.

"Yep. A nice addition to the money laundering, grand theft, and shaking down auto dealers for protection money."

"Which is racketeering?"

She nodded. Damn. I should write a paper on Casino Guy, or at least keep notes and turn them over to Colleen. It would certainly be interesting to get her take on such bravado and blatant disregard for the law. Cait and I lingered at the table after we were done eating, sipping wine and chatting about what it is that makes crime so attractive to some people. It's easy to label every criminal as an amoral sociopath, but of course, it's more complex than that in most cases. Greed, ego, and a desire for power can corrupt and skew thinking. And once they experience the rush of getting away with something, the desire to do it again—and often in a bigger way—is irresistible.

Cait decided to follow me to campus the next morning rather than riding with me so she wouldn't be stuck there all day. I'd arranged for her to chat with one of the criminal justice profs, hoping he could answer some of her questions about grand theft auto, racketeering, and the prosecution of crimes that take place in multiple states. If that didn't get her anywhere, she could also search for what she needed in the library. I had no excuse for why it had taken me so long to suggest she take advantage of the resources on campus, and she agreed that it was worth her time to see what she could turn up. It was good to see her fired up again over the past few weeks in pursuit of the story rather than worried about Daniel. I'm not used to seeing her upset, and watching her agonize over whatever trouble he may or may not have been in was hard to take, especially when there was nothing I could do to help.

27

The Other would be leaving soon, maybe for good this time. That thought filled him with sadness, but he knew it was necessary. He understood now that they couldn't stay together forever. But oh, what they'd been able to accomplish. He allowed himself a moment to revel in thoughts of their work of the past few months. His latest events had undoubtedly been his best work, and the Other was pleased. But it wasn't time to rest just yet. There was much planning to do to in order to orchestrate the finale—what was sure to be his finest effort. Each step was carefully thought out and had to be taken at just the right moment. Then it would all come together, and they'd see that he had been the smart one, the powerful one, all along, and they never should have disparaged him and told him he'd amount to nothing.

He went into the campus library and sat down at a study table. The quiet helped him focus on his plans. He even had a backpack, books, a notepad, and pen so he looked like a student. But he never wrote down any of his plans; that would be far too risky. He shuddered at the thought of a normal reading them. He was at the university quite a lot these days, wandering around as if he had as much reason to be there as anyone. He thought about how easy it had been to figure out the identity of the smarty-pants professor who was helping the cops. If she was so brilliant, how come she hadn't figured out who he was? He was right here, walking around in broad daylight, even going into her building and into her office to leave her a special gift. The normals really are dense. It's a wonder they can find their way to the bathroom.

A woman approached with an armload of books and dumped them on the table. She smiled and nodded as she sat down across from him, and he returned the gesture as if he were just another poor soul saddled with papers to write and tests to take. Well, this was an interesting turn of circumstances. An extremely opportune turn. He looked down at his notepad and suddenly had an idea. A brilliant idea. He'd have to be careful not to push too hard and to time it exactly right. Fortunately, he was very patient. He could wait all day to execute one tiny aspect of a plan. He picked up his pen and began to write, let out a breath, and stifled a giggle. What a lucky day it was turning out to be. Once again, he put his trust in the Other and watched everything fall into place. He opened a book and pretended to read and take notes.

Not quite an hour later, the woman sighed, looked at her watch, and began to gather her things. As she stacked the books she'd been reading on the edge of the table, he looked up and said, "Calling it a day?"

She nodded. "I found what I needed, so I really should get back to work."

Not in a huge hurry, that was good. That was to his advantage. But still, it wouldn't do to be careless. Now was the time for finesse. He nodded. "Well, have a good afternoon."

"Thanks, you too."

He watched her put the books she'd pulled from the stacks onto a refile cart. Oh, how very polite of her. Another girl scout like her pal, the smarty-pants professor. He rolled his eyes. When he was sure she wasn't looking his way, he grabbed his backpack, slipped the book and notepad inside, and followed her out of the library.

He tailed her through the visitor's parking lot at a safe distance. He'd learned that most normals could be followed ridiculously closely because they never expect anything like that to happen to them, and if people don't believe something will happen, they don't see it until it's too late. The woman stopped and unlocked a newer Audi TT Roadster. Not bad. Apparently, sticking your nose into other people's business pays well. He threaded his way through the vehicles in the lot and approached her as she put her bag into the car. *Appear worried but not frantic. A little vulnerable. Play the part.*

"Excuse me, sorry to bother you."

She looked up, a glimmer of recognition in her eyes. *Easy now.*

"No problem. What's up?" She rested her arm on top of the open door.

"My car won't start, and like a dope, I forgot to charge my phone this morning. Is there any way I could use yours to call Triple A? I promise it won't take long."

"Uh, sure." She leaned into the car and reached for her bag. "I've been there. Dead batteries are a drag."

He was on her in a second. One hand over her mouth, the other twisting the back of her blouse, holding the collar tight against her throat. One knee pinning her down and he bent close and whispered, "Don't scream, don't make a fuss. Do exactly as I say, and you'll live. Nod once if you understand."

She nodded, her entire body rigid and her breathing rapid. He could feel her heart was pounding like a frightened little bunny. Nope, they never see it coming.

*****

There's nothing like ending the day with a department meeting. To be fair, we're lucky. Some department chairs are an absolute pain to deal with, and Lydia is reasonable for the most part. She's approachable, open-minded, and isn't afraid to go to bat for her employees. Unfortunately, her meetings are known for going into overtime in the interest of covering every possible topic and making sure everyone who wants to have the chance to speak up gets it. Tony, Angelica, and I sat near the front and steeled ourselves for a long hour-plus. Taking her phone out of her bag, Ang said, "Turn your ringer off."

"Oh, I forgot—thanks!" I said, quickly silencing mine. Cell phones ringing in the middle of a meeting make our boss lose her temper immediately.

Lydia began the meeting, and I gave up trying to pay attention. Clinical Psych is more demanding than Psych 101 in that I'd have to do not only more reading for the class but also more reading of student papers, which would be more involved than those from the introductory class. I was trying to come up with the best way to balance that this semester but hadn't yet figured it out. Tony nudged me at one point, and I realized Lydia was looking right at me. Busted. Her spidey sense tingles when she's losing anyone in her audience. I sat up straight and gave her an encouraging smile.

An hour and seventeen minutes later, the meeting finally adjourned. I looked at my phone to check the time and saw that Cait had texted, telling me she'd gone to West Sacramento to check out a warehouse potentially full of stolen cars and that hers wouldn't start. She wanted me to come get her. I assumed she knew better than to call Jesse, who would lecture her about driving out there at night alone. I replied that I'd just gotten out of a meeting and was on my way. I headed to the faculty garage with the rest of the department. It was dark and damp, and the fog was already setting in. I said good night to my colleagues and started my car. Cait hadn't yet responded to my text. It was possible she'd lost the signal, or maybe her phone battery was as dead as her car's. I called Jesse while waiting for the car to warm up and the heat to kick in and went straight to his voice mail. I left a quick message, telling him I was on my way to get Cait. It would have been wise to wait for him, but I was worried about keeping Cait waiting.

I pulled out of the garage, going toward the south entrance of campus, wondering what Cait thought she'd be able to find after hours at a warehouse in West Sac, why she'd taken off without saying anything, and why it couldn't wait until morning. I got on Highway 50 at Howe Avenue and headed west. It got gloomier the closer I got to downtown, and I fought the sense of claustrophobia I always get driving in the fog at night. There's something about not being able to see past the little bubble of light my headlights create that freaks me out. December and January are notorious for pea soup, accident-causing fog in the valley. The Sacramento airport, which is about ten miles northwest of downtown, is situated in the middle of the rice paddies, and the fog is so thick at times planes are grounded. I came back from a conference in Los Angeles one January and was amazed we'd been able to land. After spending twenty minutes searching for my car in long-term parking, I got on I-5, irritated and shivering from the damp cold. Then I completely missed the J Street exit because visibility was so poor.

I left the freeway at Enterprise Boulevard and instantly wanted to turn around. It was dark as hell out there with no streetlights, and the warehouses looked creepy and foreboding looming out of the fog. There were no other cars around, so I slowed to a crawl, trying to find the address I was looking for. Why the hell would Cait come out here alone at night and why hadn't she or Jesse called me back yet? I finally saw a building with an address I could read and realized I'd gone too far. I flipped a U and circled back, pulling into a parking lot I assumed to be the right one. I didn't see a single car, including Cait's. I sat there idling, thinking I should just leave.

I pulled my phone out of my bag to try Cait again and saw a text from her that simply read, "Trouble. Need your help now." Holy crap. I quickly texted Jesse, telling him I was at a warehouse on Enterprise, shut off the engine, and stashed my bag in the trunk. As my eyes adjusted to the dark, I could finally see the addresses. The one I was looking for was the third building back from the street. I was already shivering in the damp cold. If Cait were here, where the hell was her car? And why did she think whatever she was onto couldn't wait until morning? I reached the building and looked around. Still no sign of life. I took a deep breath and went inside.

28

This was not good. Not good at all. Cait was nowhere to be seen, and neither was anyone else. I was in an abandoned warehouse in the deserted-after-dark industrial part of West Sac and, like an idiot, hadn't wanted to wait for Jesse. I was getting more freaked out as all of that sank in and was reaching for my phone when I heard footsteps. Reminding myself to keep breathing, I tried to disappear into the shadows of the cold, cobweb-infested corner I'd stepped into. I was calculating the distance to the doorway when the footfalls stopped. The resulting silence was even scarier. Breathe.

"It's about time you got here, Ashley. I was starting to think you weren't going to show."

What? What the hell was Ian doing here? Why would he be— *Oh good lord, no!* The killer wasn't dead after all. Ian…Ian killed all those people. *Holy shit, one of my old friends is a psychotic murderer.* I was obviously in extreme danger, but the shock nearly knocked the wind out of me. Even worse, though, was the sense of betrayal. One of my own, one of my Tower family, was a murderer. How was that even possible? I thought of how many times we'd closed together and been in the store alone after hours. How often had he walked me to my car well after midnight? Hell, I'd invited him into my home when he came to my Christmas party last month. It felt like I'd taken an icicle to the stomach.

The survival instinct is an amazing thing, and fortunately, mine kicked into high gear. I was completely stunned, but there would be plenty of time for that later. Right now, I had to concentrate on staying alive. It was obviously futile to try and reason with a completely unhinged serial killer, who was no doubt contemplating a nasty way in which he might do me in, but since I didn't have anything in my pockets except my phone and keys, not even a nail file, talking my way out of this ridiculous situation was my only chance of walking out of here.

"Ashley…," Ian sang, "it's time to come out and play…"

He was less than three feet from me, illuminated by a bare light-bulb above the door. That cliché about your life flashing before your eyes when you think you might die is just that. I saw nothing but a filthy warehouse and a spiky-haired jerk who wanted to hurt me.

Anger was good; it might well keep me in the game, but I had to be careful. Too much would push said jerk over the edge he was so precariously perched upon. And I certainly couldn't stay here all night and wait for him to leave. I took a deep breath and silently let it out. Go time. I took a tentative step forward.

"Ian, wow…fancy meeting you here," I said, failing miserably at sounding casual.

He whirled around and I flinched. He was sweaty, flushed, and holding a large butcher knife. How subtle. Though it was too dark to see, I was sure his pupils were dilated. No telling what he was on, but it was no doubt as dangerous to me as it was to him.

"*There* you are," he said, as though scolding a naughty child. "I have to say I'm losing my patience with you, young lady."

"Why are you so upset with me, Ian?" I took the tiniest step toward the door. Bad move.

"Don't even think about it!" he shouted. "You are not going anywhere!"

My autonomic nervous system was in overdrive, readying my body for flight or fight, neither of which were an option right now. If my fear kept escalating, the impulse to fight or get the hell out of there would be replaced by dissociation and I'd freeze. I needed to move, and I needed to keep Ian talking.

"Of course, I'm not leaving," I said. "You obviously have something really important to tell me, so go ahead. What's on your mind?" Despite the cold, I could feel my shirt sticking to my back.

"You think you're so smart," he said, walking toward me, "with your fancy degrees and your big-time teaching job. You know where I went to school, Ashley? The school of hard knocks. I fought for everything I have, and no one has ever handed me anything. You've been looking down on me ever since our record store days. You thought you were better than me just because you were going to college."

Speaking of clichés...I wasn't sure what Ian thought those hard knocks were, but maybe that was how I could keep him talking.

"That's not true, Ian. I knew you'd end up working for a record label, and you did. You stayed in the business. I never figured out how to do that."

"Don't lie to me," he whispered. "Sure, we used to have fun together, but I wasn't good enough for you, was I? I was never going to be anything more than a friend. Just someone to toy with."

"Come on, Ian, we flirted, but it was all in fun. You were with Cecelia, and I was with Jonathan. We both knew it was innocent."

"Bullshit. You knew I really wanted to be with you. You were such a tease." He paused, looked at the skylight, and said in a normal tone, "Hey, wasn't it supposed to rain tonight?"

What? He then continued in the angry guy voice. *Uh-oh.*

"Then you left Tower and just completely forgot about me, didn't you?"

Good lord. Ian the psychopath might indeed have dissociative identity disorder. Super. No telling how large a cast of characters there was dancing around in that fevered brain.

"Come here," he said, grabbing me by the hair.

Breathe, just keep breathing, I thought. At least, I hadn't frozen. Yet. He kept a hold of my hair and roughly pulled me toward the back of the warehouse, away from the doorway I'd come in.

"Keep moving."

"Where are we going?"

"Shut up."

There were no skylights in the back part of the warehouse, so it was getting even darker. Maybe if I concentrated on not tripping over something and breaking my neck before Ian had a chance to kill me, I might keep my brain working. I could see a little hint of light in the far right corner he seemed to be steering me toward. A window? An open door would be better, but I'd take what I could get. I felt a draft of cold air as we got closer to the corner and saw that one of the big roll-up doors that lined the back wall was open. That was just cruel. So close.

"Sit down."

I was clearly in big trouble. Ian had been here earlier, setting up his next gruesome scenario, and apparently this one was to star me. He'd put one of those giant wooden spools used to store industrial wire on its side, laid a burlap sack on top, and set two oil barrels next to it. There was a wilted bunch of wildflowers stuffed into a paper cup next to a little Coleman lantern that cast a weak pool of light on the makeshift tabletop. How cozy. I sat on one of the barrels and watched him sit on the other, wondering if he'd set down the knife. Nope. He started laughing, a high-pitched near giggle that was far more chilling than the angry guy persona or the knife.

"Well, well, we're actually on a date, Ashley. I'm finally getting what I want. Aren't you sorry you put me off for so many years? I chose this place especially for you."

"You sure do know how to impress a lady, Ian."

"Don't be a smart-ass. Put your phone on the table and anything else you have in your pockets."

I complied, not taking my eyes off him. I desperately hoped my phone was still in silent mode, fearing he'd lose it completely if it chimed with incoming texts from Jesse or Cait. Speaking of Jesse, where the hell was he? And Cait? If she were here somewhere...if he'd done something to her... I couldn't even complete that thought. I noticed a phone in front of him, and when he saw me glance at it, he said, "Aren't you a good friend to come all this way on a dark, foggy night to rescue poor Caitlyn? Oh, didn't she tell you she lost her phone?" The high-pitched giggle again. I tried to concentrate on slowing my heartbeat, telling myself that Cait was fine, that he'd just gotten a hold of her phone somehow to get me to come down here. Then I noticed his black eye.

"Nice shiner, Ian."

He glared at me. "Your friend needs to learn some manners."

I suppressed a grin. *Well done, Cait.* Apparently, Ian didn't know much about her background or how she'd earned her Pulitzer.

"But she was just a means to an end. Just a step to get to you. Once I was sure you were coming, I was done with her."

Done with her? My heart started pounding again, and my stomach lurched. *Stay calm. Breathe.* I'd be no use to Cait dead. I'd talk my way out of this ridiculous game and find her. Or Jesse would. She was fine…she had to be.

Ian swept his free hand toward two flasks sitting by the lantern. Things were about to get even weirder.

"Since this is our first date, I wasn't sure whether to go with red or white."

His shrill laughter echoed off the cinder block walls again. He clearly wasn't talking about wine.

"So you have your choice. The red is a genuinely nice automatic transmission fluid, vintage last month, I believe. And the white is an exquisitely crafted brake fluid that's been aged to perfection."

I stared at him as he toyed with the knife.

"Now I could make you drink both right away and watch you get violently ill and then die, but what fun would that be? So we're going to play a little game instead."

Awesome. My date from hell with an actual psychopath was going to include a game. I took slow, even breaths, trying to convince myself that if I could make him think I was going to play his little game, I could stay alive. Maybe it was as simple as that.

"You think you've been so clever, helping your detective pal figure out all of the clues I've left, but they were so easy, really elementary stuff if you have half a brain. Once I realized you were the so-called *expert*"—he spat out the word as though it left a bitter taste—"lending a hand, I should have made them harder. After all, I wouldn't want to insult your intelligence. So my gift to you, sweet little Ashley, is an exceedingly difficult, obscure reference that will really put you to the test. Your cop pals wouldn't get it in a million years. It's my best effort, if I do say so myself. And because I'm feeling charitable, I'll give you three guesses."

He was sweating again, and his hands were shaking. I opened my mouth, but no sound emerged. I coughed and tried again.

"Sounds fun, Ian. I...I like games..."

"Oh, you'll love this one. You get three guesses, but each time you guess wrong, you have to take a little sip from one of the flasks. Ready? Go!" He slapped his left hand on the spool. I flinched. I feared I would hyperventilate, and I was clenching my teeth so hard I was getting a headache. I forced myself to breathe normally. I didn't really think psychopaths could smell fear like dogs, but you never know. I had to keep him talking. I had no flipping idea what his twisted brain had cooked up for our date scenario, but I needed to think of something and damned quickly. 'The Sad Café' by the Eagles was all I could come up with, but that was too easy.

"Oh, and just to make things fair, I'll give you a little hint and tell you that the playing field is wide open. The answer I'm looking for could be from a song, a TV show, or a movie. Why limit it to just one category?" He gave me a creepy wink.

That was a hint? My mind raced. *Think about what Ian likes.* Corny sitcoms, over-the-top action adventure movies, and Southern rock and roll, like Lynyrd Skynyrd and the Allman Brothers. Crap. That sort of music not being my cup of tea, this charming café scene he'd created could be described in some obscure album cut I've never heard. Given how long he's been a part of the music world, it was a safe bet he'd stuck with a song reference and only mentioned movies and television to throw me off.

"Come on, Ashley, the clock is ticking. What's the matter? Is this one too hard? Am I too clever for you? Do you need another hint?"

He took a little toy car out of his jacket pocket and set it on the table with a flourish. It was a red VW van. What the hell did that have to do with a café?

"Well?"

"I'm just taking the time to appreciate your artistry here, Ian."

"Bullshit. Put your hands on the table. No, flat on the table in front of you."

I did as asked and watched him shift the knife in his hand so the blade was sticking out from the bottom of his fist. He placed the point between the thumb and index finger of my left hand.

"Time's up. I want your first guess. Now."

I heard a freight train approaching in the distance, the churning of the wheels pounding out a low bass rhythm.

He muttered, "Oh, and there's the train…"

Was the train another clue? A VW van, a train, a café…what the hell was it? He raised the knife and held it over my hand.

"You're taking too long. You just forfeited one guess. Take a drink." He set a flask in front of me. I picked it up, took a deep breath, and looked him in the eye. If this asshole was going to take me down, he was in for the fight of his life.

Very quickly, I glanced to my left and then back. He cocked his head, presumably trying to decide if I was playing him. I didn't have to work too hard at looking worried. He took the bait and glanced to his right, and then I threw the flask at his face, catching him on the bridge of the nose. He roared with pained surprise.

"You bitch! You'll pay for that!"

I jumped up but wasn't quite fast enough to avoid the swipe of the knife as it slashed into my upper left arm. I yelped and charged at him, figuring I had a few seconds before he brought the knife back toward me again. I hit him with everything I had, driving my elbow into his throat and knocking him off the barrel. He hit the floor with a thud I hoped knocked the wind out of him, and the knife clattered on the cement. I desperately looked around for something to hit him with. I was sure he wouldn't stay down long enough for me to grab my phone and call for help.

I'd hurt him, but I was hurt too. I could feel the blood seeping into my sleeve, and I nearly screamed when I put my hand over the wound to try to slow the bleeding. Hopefully, the pain would keep me from passing out from fear. Ian had recovered enough to crawl and was feeling his way across the floor, looking for the knife, when I kicked him in the head. He wavered but didn't go down. Good lord, what was he on? I kicked him again, this time in the ribs, and he flopped onto his back and swore at me until he went hoarse. He rolled onto his side and attempted to get up. We both spotted the knife, but I reached it first and kicked it into the darkness.

"That wasn't nice, bitch."

"Ian," I said, straining to catch my breath, "let's just get out of here, okay?"

"Who's Ian?" The maniacal laugh again. I was getting tired of his cast of lunatics.

He staggered to his feet, staring at me, and I realized he was right in front of the roll-up door that opens to the loading dock. *Does that dock extend outside? Or do the trucks back up right against the building?* A slim chance of escaping this nightmare was starting to materialize, but it felt so flimsy, like such a long shot, I was afraid if I tried too hard to grab it, it would disappear like smoke. Ian was having trouble staying on his feet, weaving like a boxer about to hit the canvas. He blinked and squinted at me.

"You ruined my game… You always have to ruin everything…"

"Ian…"

He tried to focus on me. I kept my voice soft and took slow, deliberate steps toward him. I couldn't yet see the edge of the dock.

"Why don't we start over? This hasn't been much of a date, has it? We could go get something to eat. Are you hungry?"

"You don't want to go anywhere with me. You never have, and now you're hanging out with that cop. You're hooking up with him, aren't you, Ashley?"

"No, we're just working together, we're not dating. That would be weird. I've known him since he was a kid. He's my best friend's younger brother."

He sighed. "You really need to stop lying to me."

I was finally close enough to see that there was no loading dock outside the building. Ian didn't seem to realize he was less than a foot from the edge of a five-foot drop. I took another careful step toward him.

"Come on, Ian, let's call a truce, sit down, and talk this through. What do you say?" I raised my open hands toward my shoulders in the universal gesture of meaning no harm. He started to say something, but I didn't give him the chance. I charged forward and shoved him with all my remaining strength, my arm screaming. He looked aghast, hovering for a slow-motion second and wildly waving his arms, and then toppled off the edge of the loading dock and hit the pavement below. He wouldn't be getting up.

"That's for Cody, you bastard."

My arm was throbbing. I took off my blood-soaked sweatshirt and wrapped it around the wound as best I could. I grabbed my keys and the phones, hurrying toward the front of the warehouse and the psychological safety of my car. I wanted to get the hell out of that creepy building before I passed out from blood loss, fear, or both. But where was Cait? Was she here somewhere? What had Ian meant by "done with her"? I checked her phone and found the texts he'd sent pretending to be her. How had he gotten her phone? Judging by his blackened eye, she hadn't given it up easily. I reached my car and leaned against it while I dialed 911. Once I was assured that an ambulance and patrol unit were on the way, I dialed Jesse to tell him where I was, seeing that he'd been calling and texting me for the past twenty minutes.

I was shivering from the cold, but that was nerves too, as my adrenaline slowly stopped surging. I sat in my car to wait for the paramedics, trying not to bleed all over the seat. Jesse arrived before the ambulance. When I tried to tell him what happened, it came out all jumbled, and I realized I wasn't making sense.

"You can tell me all about it later," he said, crouching down to talk to me. "I'm just so relieved I found you—I couldn't even see this building from the street. Oh shit, is that blood? Are you okay? What happened?"

"Knife fight with a psycho. I think I least slowed the bleeding."

"Good lord. Well, the ambulance will be here any minute. What on earth made you come out here by yourself?"

"I got a text I thought was from Cait saying she needed me to come get her. Do you know where she is? Is she okay? We have to find her—"

"She's fine. She's safe and sound at my place. And now we know why the killer wanted her phone. He assaulted her in the visitor's lot at the university today, but she got away when he tried to force her into his car. Guess he's not smart enough to know better than to mess with a veteran war zone reporter."

I smiled despite my pain and rattled nerves.

"Cait didn't realize she'd lost her phone in the struggle until after campus security took her to the health center to be checked out. And of course, she didn't know who had jumped her until I got there."

"But she's okay?" I needed to hear him say it again.

"A little shaken and a few bruises, but yeah, she's fine. My sister is tough."

I swooned with relief. "Yeah, I know. And so does Ian." Not that his black eye bothered him now. We heard the siren in the distance slowly growing louder.

A West Sac patrol unit arrived, and the officers leapt from the car and shouted at Jesse to get away from me. He calmly stood, hands raised, and identified himself as a homicide detective. They reluctantly stood down when he badged them. I struggled to be coherent. I handed Cait's phone to Jesse and said, "I *was* supposed to be his next victim."

"Which is why I've been franticly trying to find you since about an hour ago when I realized the guy in the river couldn't be the killer."

I was getting dizzy, even sitting down. "You did? How…how did you know?"

"The man in the river was left-handed. I might have gotten stuck with the paperwork on this case, but I went through every damned line. His name rang a vague bell, so I looked him up. He played varsity baseball in college, where he was the star left-handed pitcher."

"Wow. That's quite impressive, Detective. I…um…did you…" I needed to ask Jesse something but couldn't form the words. I wondered how much blood I'd lost.

"It's okay, we can talk about all of this later. Save your strength."

The ambulance finally arrived, and Jesse asked where Ian was. I pointed toward the railroad tracks that ran behind the warehouse with my good arm. He asked for my keys and said he'd take care of my car. *Huh?* Oh, right, I wasn't going to be driving away. I asked him to get my bag out of the trunk. Detective Marquez and an officer I didn't recognize pulled up as the EMTs were taking my vitals. They covered me with a blanket, got me loaded into the ambulance, and went about stopping the bleeding. My arm was on fire, and tears ran down my cheeks. Then it came to me—the red VW van, the nearby railroad tracks, and Ian's comment about getting what he wanted. It wasn't a café; it was a restaurant. Ian's obscure reference was Arlo Guthrie's 'Alice's Restaurant.'

I win, asshole, I thought. *Who's the clever one now?* Then I passed out.

EPILOGUE

Detective Malone was recognized for his outstanding police work and received an accommodation. I'm sure he'll move up quickly within the department. He still checks in from time to time, but we don't see much of each other anymore. The nasty gash on my arm required twenty stitches but healed well. The scar doesn't bother me because it reminds me of the strength and courage I can summon when necessary. I didn't speak publicly about my role in the investigation and refused to give interviews, but as Jesse suggested before I'd even decided to get involved, I came away with a new perspective and quite a bit of data on psychopathic behaviors as well as personal experience with the subject being charming, manipulative, and narcissistic. The resulting research paper was well received, which allowed me to take a bit of a breather from the publish-or-perish game. The success of said paper may or may not have led to the decision to offer my pop culture class during spring semester as well as fall, but it doesn't really matter. I'll take the win.

Cait's story exposed Evan's scheme to defraud his partner as well as their company, which resulted in the complete exoneration of Daniel. Evan was charged with a litany of crimes, including money laundering, grand theft auto, and embezzlement. It seems Cait and Daniel are on again, at least for the time being. She sent me a postcard from Greece. One other thing of note: Stephen and I have been spending more time together. Will that lead us to something more than friendship? It might, which would be wonderful, but if it doesn't, that's okay too. Facing death and walking away made me appreciate more than ever the fact that life really is about the journey rather than the destination and whom we invite to accompany us on that journey. And the Shelby? I'm thinking about it...

ABOUT THE AUTHOR

Denise McDonald is a copywriter, blogger, and freelance writer. Her passion for writing and creating stories began soon after her lifelong love of books was ignited at age five with her first library card. She spent her formative years at Tower Books, discovering that "too many books" is a relative term and realizing bookseller isn't just something one does; it's something one is. A native Californian, she lives in Sacramento with plenty of books and music and just enough cats. *An Advanced Degree in Murder* is her first novel.

CPSIA information can be obtained
at www.ICGtesting.com
Printed in the USA
LVHW040149271222
735905LV00002B/191